From the author of
Trusting Claire

WANTING AIDAN

ALYSSA HALL

 FriesenPress

Suite 300 - 990 Fort St
Victoria, BC, V8V 3K2
Canada

www.friesenpress.com

Portrait photo courtesy of Sasha Primak - Primus Studio
www.sashaprimak.ca

ISBN
978-1-03-910481-5 (Hardcover)
978-1-03-910480-8 (Paperback)
978-1-03-910482-2 (eBook)

1. FICTION, MYSTERY & DETECTIVE, PRIVATE INVESTIGATORS

Distributed to the trade by The Ingram Book Company

The blade sings to me. Faintly, so soft against my ears, its voice calms my worries and tells me that one touch will take it all away. It tells me that I just need to slide a long horizontal cut, and make a clean slice. It tells me the words that I have been begging to hear: this will make it okay.

Amanda Steele

CHAPTER 1

Joe Parrott woke up with a headache. The throb had settled somewhere behind his sinuses, deep in his skull. He slowly turned away from the sun shining on his face then gradually tried to open his heavy eyes. It must be past seven a.m. if the sun was already this far over. Joe was no longer accustomed to waking up with headaches as he had given up binge drinking years ago. So this one must be from the chaff and dust in the barn. He had spent the previous afternoon helping George unload a truck full of hay for the sheep farm run by his parents.

Getting out of bed, Joe made his way to the kitchen to put on some coffee, waking himself up with a few deep-breathing exercises. These were getting easier as his ribs were healing from his accident. When he passed the side door at the kitchen entranceway, he unconsciously stooped to check the bottom of his boots that were on the mat. It startled him that he did that, as it had happened weeks ago and it had taken him almost two weeks to get a decent night's sleep after the incident. Wasn't that memory behind him now?

It was nearly three weeks ago, and on that evening he had come home late after indulging in a few pints while watching a football match at the pub. It was a big game and Sheffield had won in a brilliant finish. Joe hadn't been quite that inebriated in years, and his head was in a bit of a fog when he went to bed that night. He woke up the following morning lying on top of the covers fully clothed. He had been sluggish to come downstairs to the kitchen, his head throbbing. At that time, as the wounds from his accident were more recent, he was moving considerably slower. It was while the coffee was brewing that he saw the mat stained with darkening blood from the bottom of his boots.

Joe felt ill. He remembered that feeling right now. When he had opened the door to take the bloodstained boots outside, he eyed the browning boot prints coming from the direction of his parked car. But even if he had been drunk he was surprised he hadn't noticed them, as the prints gained in thickness as he followed the trail from his front step. He had tracked the prints to an area beside the driver's door of his vehicle, where he spotted a pool of cracking, blackened solid matter. Did he do something that he couldn't remember? Surely he didn't hit anything on his way home. A careful inspection revealed there was no blood on the actual car, nor anywhere inside.

It was at that moment he heard the flies. He turned and then noticed the body in the low shrub not six feet from where he stood. The ground was on enough of a downward slope to cause the blood to creep towards the vehicle. Joe stood looking down at her, staring in disbelief. He couldn't make out the face except for the nose bent into the dirt, mixed with thick once crimson blood that had become crusted and black around the head. And the one eye that seemed focused on his boot as if saying something about him walking in her blood.

In a state of shock Joe had returned to the house and dialed 999. He had stayed inside until the police arrived, afraid to touch anything outside. His headache had grown in intensity. His friend DI Harry Wilkes was the first to arrive. A forensics team followed shortly after. Joe had spent the next two hours answering questions and retracing his steps from the previous evening. He had left home at seven p.m. and been at the pub for three hours before coming straight home. The attending coroner believed that the girl had been murdered somewhere around eight, based on the condition of the body. Once the coroner had finished his inquiries, the team had left, taking his boots along with the body.

The coroner assured Joe the woman would not have been alive when he got home. Even so, Joe felt he might have had a chance to save her had he been sober. Although consumed with guilt the man said it was a wasted emotion. She could not have been saved as most of her blood had drained from her body. A mass of tissue was protruding from the right side of the girl's neck where her carotid and jugular had been slit. This explained the sheer amount of blood at the scene.

Joe was a private investigator, and while he was no stranger to criminal activity, murder was not familiar territory. Finding a body so close to his home had a profound effect on him. Even with the passage of time, he still felt rattled at the mental image of the corpse, the greatest impact being that it was a young woman. Did a man kill her? A man should never do this to a woman.

After weeks of sleepless nights, he was gradually returning to normal. It all came flashing back to him this morning as for some unknown reason he had looked at bottom of his shoes. It was an impulsive response to that past traumatic event, but why now? After splashing water on his face, Joe returned to the kitchen to pour his coffee. He cursed as the rancid milk curdled in his mug. Dumping everything down the drain, he went to the bedroom to dress. Not a good start to the day. The headache had miraculously disappeared as he grappled with the issue of the coffee. He needed to go buy milk, although this was the last thing he felt like doing. Grabbing his sweater and his keys, he left the house, squinting in the sunlight.

"Good morning Joe," hollered his neighbor Rob from across the street.

Joe kept his head down and pretended not to hear, quickly getting into his car to avoid a conversation.

"That's the last thing I want right now," he mumbled under his breath. He was well aware of his shortcomings, idle chat with inquisitive neighbours being one of them. Rob had lived in the house across the street for perhaps ten years. Early efforts at conversation had been futile. Joe knew that a neighbor doesn't necessarily become a friend and such was the case here. Where was it written that he needed to bond with this person? He felt bad ignoring Rob today but he felt himself sinking into despondency all over again.

While driving the short distance to Co-op Foods, he spontaneously turned in the opposite direction and instead headed to Nonna's Café on Ecclesall Road. He had a good chance of catching his friend Simon there and by doing so, taking his mind off the events of this morning. Sure enough, as he approached the building he viewed Simon through the front window. He was seated just inside the door on his usual bar stool, facing the street, his face buried in the morning paper.

CHAPTER 2

Looking up from his paper, Simon waved Joe over. "Good morning, mate. I'm just reading about the victory party last night. I'm happy to see that David Cameron is in for another term. So maybe we can get going with his idea of a referendum. Let's get this country on the right track. What say you, Joe?"

"Good for the Prime Minister, Simon." Joe's mind was miles away but it was good to sit here with his mate.

The two men sat with their coffees, Simon still in conversation about David Cameron's victory at the polls.

"And I see our MP Miss Haigh kept her seat, so all is as it should be. The markets opened strong this morning, which is a good sign. Right?"

Simon looked over to Joe and said, "Hey mate, are you even listening to me? You seem miles away."

"I'm sorry Simon. It's just troubling about the shoes. Why today after all this time would I look at the bottom of my shoes?"

"Who can ever explain the way the brain works. Have you heard any more about the girl?" Simon spoke the words although his tone lacked any real concern and his eyes were still scanning his paper.

"No not yet. I will call David at the station on Monday," Joe commented more to himself than to Simon.

"So I hear Susan's finished uni and heading home?" was Simon's effort to change the conversation.

"Yes, she's finally moving back here to Sheffield. They move into their new flat in a fortnight and Nigel is expecting her this weekend to see how things are going. I promised him we'd make it a bit presentable before she arrives."

"Must be good for you, she's not been here for quite some time, not even for a visit."

It was true. His daughter, Susan, hadn't been home to see Joe much in the past year and a half as she had been attending Manchester University where she was studying to become a vet. But now that her boyfriend Nigel had decided to open a new practice in Sheffield, it wasn't long before Susan agreed to move in with him, and they promptly rented a flat in Hunters Bar.

Joe's daughter, Susan, now a very grown up twenty-three, had lived in Manchester with her mom Janet for the past six years ever since Joe and Janet divorced. Janet had generously suggested Joe keep the family house so that Susan could come 'home' when she visited her dad. Theirs was a good relationship all around, and both Susan and Janet had visited Joe often over the years, hiking together and sharing meals. The damage from their bad marriage could never be repaired but there remained a lingering love between them.

Susan's boyfriend, Nigel, whom she met in university, had recently become a farm animal vet and was excited to have the opportunity to set up his practice. Susan chose domestic animals as her specialty and there was little doubt she would be busy before long. These days it seems everyone owned a dog or two, and a couple of cats as well.

Joe stood up. "Yes, it's been awhile. I have to run, Simon. I need to buy milk then go over to see Nigel. I am helping him unload a truck full of furnishings."

"Alright then, I'm off as well. Can't sit here all day now, can I?" followed Simon.

The men left the café together and said goodbye outside.

"Simon, you need to buy new shoes. They still squeak, man. What's wrong with you?" Joe yelled. But Simon was already walking away and he merely raised his hand in the air in a disinterested fashion and carried on down the walk. Joe shook his head in bewilderment. Simon's self-care had become quite appalling. He regularly either needed a haircut or had a button missing from his shirt, or was sporting a mustard stain down the front of his sweater.

Simon was his mate through the school years, having met at Hunters Bar School at the start of Year 4 when they were eight years old. Simon had latched on to Joe on his first day, loving the idea of having an American Brit for a best friend. Their friendship continued through their secondary years at Silverdale School and into adulthood. Joe was not accustomed to seeing his friend this way. He was trying to remember exactly when Simon's hygiene had begun to diminish.

Glancing at his watch, Joe decided to walk to Nigel's. By the time he stopped for groceries and found a new parking spot he may be late. Parking around Hunters Bar had become atrocious over the past few years. Where the hell did everyone come from? Walking up the hill he decided to take Pinner Road to Penrhyn where the newly rented row house was situated. The walk took Joe just over ten minutes. Up ahead he could see Nigel's truck parked and on the footway he could see him standing with another person. A shock of blonde hair and a habit of doing a little foot dance when she was excited, which she obviously was now, made her instantly recognizable. Susan must have driven down very early this morning. Counter-surprise - the place would be a mess.

Joe whistled as he approached them, and Susan looked up and waved, breaking into a smile.

"Hullo Dad," she called. Joe gave his daughter a proper hug, almost smothering her small frame. She was not quick to let go, reinforcing how much she had missed him. Susan seemed to have grown so much since he last saw her. Although they spoke regularly on Skype, it wasn't the same as seeing her in person. She had blossomed somehow, having evolved over the past four years from disconsolate to exultant. Their divorce had been a difficult and challenging time for his daughter, but Nigel breathed new life into her.

It took under an hour for the three of them to unload Nigel's truck, allowing for plenty of laughter and feigned grunting by the two men. They handled the few pieces of heavy furniture while Susan carried in a dozen boxes, seemingly more interested in what was in them rather than simply getting them off the truck. The men navigated around the box lids strewn around the sitting room. The flat still looked ingloriously bare but Susan showed every sign of being perfectly pleased with their meager progress.

She stood back to take it all in. "It's going to be fabulous, look at these windows!"

"Don't worry, love, I'll have the rest moved over before you get back," promised Nigel.

Susan squeezed his hand gently before turning to her dad. "Are you up for a hike?" she suggested. "I'm here until Wednesday. It might do you good to get that body moving again. We can take it slow and maybe head over to Derbyshire? Nigel and I thought it would be a nice change, he knows I've been talking about it for months. I was thinking we could then grab a pint at Fox House before heading back. I've been cooped up and I can't wait to get onto the moors."

"That's a splendid idea, you're on," was Joe's immediate reply. It was indeed a splendid idea.

CHAPTER 3

Joe's impatience had grown considerably by Monday. He was eager for some answers about the murder victim. He took it as an omen that he had looked at his shoes last Friday so today he planned on calling in at the police station to see if they could tell him something about the young woman. As a Private Investigator, he had good connections due to the nature of his work. Joe's old school friend David, now a constable with the South Yorkshire Police Department, was great at giving him intel and keeping him in the loop. Before Joe had become a PI, he and David had occasions to share information during Joe's years in security. His cases had often been linked to crimes.

Joe headed out a little before noon. He stopped at the morgue on his way to the police station. He was hoping there had been a breakthrough as to who she was. The girl has been on ice for the past three weeks pending identification. After greeting Ganesh, Joe followed him down the stairs at the end of the hall. Ganesh Bhatti was the senior coroner, whom Joe also knew through his work. He led Joe into his working area. A body on a gurney covered with a sheet was visible through the large glass window. Ganesh picked up the file that was lying on his table.

"Is that her?" Joe asked.

"Yes, I'm just relocating her and changing the Jane Doe tag to add a proper name." Ganesh had removed a sheet of paper from the folder. "I have good news for you, Joe. The girl has been identified. As you know, we were waiting for her fingerprints to be run through the database. Then three days ago the police received a missing person's report. Bloke who runs the Nether Edge Hotel called police to say he was missing an employee, a young woman named Rita. She had been living on the premises but he's not seen hide nor hair of her for a while."

Ganesh went on to say that the brief description from the man, combined with today's results from the fingerprint database confirmed that this was indeed the same person.

"Okay, so our victim is Rita Nowak, I'd peg her at approximately twenty-four years old. I didn't find any defensive marks on the body, which means either she knew her assailant or he really surprised her and she didn't have a chance to react. Also, not sure I should be telling you this, but she's had a baby. There's a C-section scar but we have no knowledge of any children at this point. What I mean is, nobody's called to say mummy's gone missing. Hard to say how old the scar is. I'd say more than six years ago."

"If that's the case, she'd have been, what? Around sixteen when she had the baby? That's fairly young, I'd say."

"Yes, although I can't say with any certainty how old the scar is but I do know it's not recent. Police are searching for next of kin. Also, she has a small tattoo that might be traceable. It may tell us something more about her, like where she's been."

"Tattoo?"

"Yes, a tiny turtle, upper arm just above the elbow."

Joe wanted to help this poor soul who had lay twisted, her face staring at his boot. Although this was not his case, his curiosity had been piqued. His concern, while inexplicable, was absolute. "Thanks, Ganesh, I appreciate the update. I'm heading over to see David at the police station now. He can fill me in on anything else."

He stopped at the door and turned to have one more look at the white sheet silhouetting the body before leaving the building. How tragic. This young woman had suddenly become an insignificant shape under a sheet in the morgue.

Seeing the expression on his face, Ganesh called after him. "Hey Joe… she bled out, man. You couldn't have done anything."

Nodding reluctantly in concession, Joe left the building. He then drove the short distance to the station, where he didn't need to wait long for David to greet him. He was ushered into his cubicle where he received more detail. A further search revealed that Rita had been reported missing eight years ago by London Police.

"Eight years? Why had she not been found earlier? Especially since she was right here in Yorkshire. That's a lot of time gone by. It's like someone stopped looking."

David replied, "People disappear all the time, Joe, for every possible reason. Some cases are solved but more are not. Did you know there's approximately 100,000 people go missing in the UK every year? This was from a report I read. Missing People charity puts these out regularly. It's only because she's dead and has a criminal file that we were able to track her down, but otherwise she's would have been another to slip through the cracks. Besides Joe, she's of legal age, so nobody would be looking any longer."

"So, the family's only hope was that the girl would eventually have made her way back home," added Joe. "So who was the bloke who reported her missing?"

"His name is Thomas King and he's the proprietor at the Nether Edge Hotel. We haven't been over to see him yet." David glanced at the information on his desk as he continued, "I gave them a call down in London, and I found a sergeant who had the file. She called me back pretty quickly and filled me in on what she had. Rita was the daughter of a Polish woman named Lena Nowak who lives in a housing estate in Dagenham. Mrs. Nowak would call Sergeant Walters from time to time to see if there has been any news but over the years the calls have understandably become less frequent." He moved some papers around his desk just as his phone rang.

"Call me in a day or two, Joe. Our people in London will call Mrs. Nowak, as they know the case. Sergeant Walters says she'll get back to me as soon as she can. Says she's not looking forward to the call. Mrs. Nowak will be dashed. I guess a mother always has hope her daughter will come home."

"Thanks, David, I'll call you soon," Joe replied as he stood, leaving the man to take his call. Joe gave him a nod and he headed for the door, knowing he would be planning a trip to the Nether Edge.

On his way to the exit he ran into DI Wilkes who at that moment was heading out of the building.

"Are you here about the girl, Joe?"

"I am, Harry. Just doing a bit of digging on my own. I just heard she was reported missing." Joe noticed a bit of an enthusiastic lilt to his own voice, which caught him by surprise. Although still officially on injury leave he was feeling more than ready to get back to work. Seven weeks was far too long to be off the job.

"Just don't get in the way of our investigation, Joe. That's all I ask," Harry called after him. "And keep us in the loop!" Harry was not a fool and had a good idea that Joe would indeed be getting involved. He looked out the window and was not surprised to see Joe's car do a U-turn and head in the general direction of the Nether Edge Hotel.

Joe and Harry respected each other. One of Joe's first cases back when he was starting out had involved asset tracing, where the suspect was found in his car with a bullet hole in his forehead. Joe had been introduced to DI Wilkes who was investigating the murder. Given that Joe had already learned so much about the people involved, Harry found him to be a valuable source of information. The two men had hit it off and their working relationship became established. Between David and DI Wilkes, Joe's network was strong.

CHAPTER 4

A crisp sunny morning greeted Joe as he walked across the front room to the kitchen to make his coffee. His trip to visit the proprietor at the hotel had been disappointing, as the man was not there when Joe arrived. He had apparently gone to visit his brother in Stafford. Joe had managed to schedule a visit for two days forward, making it clear to the person on the phone that he was not the police. But today he would put it out of his mind, as today was his day to ramble with Susan and Nigel.

Being Tuesday, the hiking trails would be less busy than on a weekend. Susan and Nigel arrived promptly at ten. He had been tying his boots when they climbed the steps to the front door, hats and water in hand. Within minutes the three of them set off for their trek. The route took them from Fulwood along Porter Brook on Clough Lane. Then crossing the pastureland up to Ringinglow they continued along the old Roman Road to Fox House. The seemingly endless sweep of moors was densely blanketed in purple heather. The patchwork green of the verdant fields was patterned by the low dry stone walls which stretched across the landscape in a myriad of curved patterns.

These field boundary walls were built without mortar or cement and covered thousands of miles of land across the moors. Many were built over four hundred years ago and would likely last four hundred more. On the horizon, the tors, or rock outcrops, were etched into the endless blue sky that was visible from every direction.

Susan walked ahead, placing Joe between her and Nigel, who was very chatty this morning. His love of animals was apparent while he described his first few farm visits as the new local veterinarian. It was lambing season and it was a good time to be making himself known in the area. During lambing, there were many things that could go wrong, either with the delivery or afterwards, and Nigel was making Joe aware of all of them, despite the fact that Joe had been lambing with his father for years. Joe remained silent, but for a few affirmative grunts. He appreciated Nigel's chatter as his thoughts were elsewhere.

"Will Carole be working today, Dad?" Susan asked over her shoulder, bringing Joe's thoughts back to the present. Carole was Joe's girlfriend. He wouldn't call her a girlfriend although they have been seeing each other for nearly two years. It was Joe who kept the distance between them, not wanting a complicated relationship at this stage of his life.

"I imagine she will be there today, love. She'll be chuffed to see you. We weren't expecting you for another few weeks."

Susan smiled at this. "I like surprising people, especially Carole. She'll turn red and make that little noise she always makes."

Joe smiled as he let Nigel pass him so he could walk with Susan for a spell.

They continued in silence, accompanied only by the sounds of bleating sheep resounding over the moors. Underfoot were the occasional remnants of cobblestone, presumably left by the Romans when they built this road. Joe was not surprised that Susan had chosen this hike; it had always been her favourite as a child. He had many fond memories of the three of them setting off on their Sunday constitutional, discussing their previous week and upcoming plans. Looking at Susan walking now with Nigel, Joe was reminded of Janet back in the carefree days. He had lost her as a wife but was more than grateful to still have her as a friend. Although Joe saw a lot of himself in his daughter she was definitely more Janet.

Joe's ex-wife, Janet, had moved to Manchester following their split, to take a promotion as head of pediatrics at Royal Manchester Hospital. She had worked most of her nursing career in maternity and had trained very hard at grooming herself for this position, with Joe's support. He spent the bulk of the time at home with a young Susan while Janet finished her degree. Once the official news came, they had celebrated into the wee hours. As a couple they had always been extremely supportive of each other's dreams and goals - the difference being that Janet actually had dreams and goals.

The former Janet Parrott now sported the new name of Janet Lawson, having recently married a doctor named Alan Lawson. Dr. Lawson was a surgeon, two years younger than Janet and an avid cyclist. He was fiercely committed to their careers and to the marriage. Joe could see how happy she was. This was the change she needed from what he had offered her, which was gritty work, long hours, and too many pub nights. Alan was a great guy and the two men got along well.

It was about nine months ago that Joe had driven to Manchester to attend the small celebration. His mother had disapproved of his involvement but his enthusiasm would not have kept him away. It was also the first time that he had met Nigel. Susan was tickled that the men shared something in common. They both had fathers who were born overseas, namely North America. Nigel's father was born in Toronto, Canada. Joe and Nigel had tried to explain to her that it might as well be Manchester and Munich as there was a big disparity between Seattle and Toronto.

They were married outdoors on a sunny afternoon. Both bride and groom were informally dressed in matching biscuit-coloured linens. Janet's dress was simple and mid-calf length, Alan's shirt casually worn untucked. The ceremony was brief and uplifting with simple vows that the pair had written themselves, Alan's being humorous enough to challenge Billy Connolly himself. It was a happy occasion and Joe was a model ex-husband, sober and keenly involved in the event. Susan barely left his side, openly proud that her dad had chosen to be a part of the family, and always would be.

Joe's mom, Emma, had never taken to Janet. She felt she was too cheerful.

"Nobody right in the head is that cheerful all the time. There's just no reason for it," she had said on more than one occasion.

Joe could never make sense of that line of thinking. And his mother felt that Janet was an irresponsible mother as well.

"A mother's place is with her child, not trotting off after a career," was Emma's other major criticism of her daughter-in-law.

As the three of them neared Fox House, Joe asked Susan how her mum was adjusting to the new marriage and the job. "I hope to see her for your birthday next month, she's let me know they are coming."

"She's hunky-dory, Dad. I'll tell her you said hullo. She'll be happy to know that you have healed so well. You really gave us all a fright. Did you ever catch the man?"

"Not yet, Susan. And maybe never. Even if I recognize him I couldn't place him at the scene after all this time."

"It's not fair, people getting away with things like this," was her answer.

Joe was enjoying the walk but not so much this new topic. He let out a huge sigh of relief as over the ridge, the inn came into view. This was good timing and he found he was looking forward to seeing Carole. His mind had definitely been drifting away from Susan and Nigel and he was trying hard to not make it obvious. He intended to finish off this visit with his daughter in high fashion and this timely pub stop would help.

CHAPTER 5

Following up with David a few days later, Joe entered the station carrying two cups of coffee. David received confirmation earlier that the London police had contacted Mrs. Nowak. Joe was informed that a Constable Jane Walters was the file officer on the case. She said she and Rita's mom had spoke at length.

"Walters said the woman was beside herself, screaming and all."

How Rita had avoided detection for so many years was a mystery to Joe. Then again, as David had said, it can be difficult finding someone who doesn't want to be found, even for the police.

"The mum says she can't believe her daughter ended up in Sheffield. I mentioned that it was you who found Rita, and now she's keen to know who you are. She'd like to talk to you, Joe. Here, I've written the number down," said David as he handed Joe a piece of paper. "I know you'd be hunting her down as soon as you walked out of here anyways. I thought I'd spare you the trouble."

Joe thanked David. He wanted nothing more than to have a conversation with this woman. Having discovered the body and feeling he could have saved her, he felt oddly responsible. He took the piece of paper that David handed him and tucked it into his pocket. "Thanks, David, I really appreciate this," he said as he warmly shook the man's hand. Joe walked out into the sunlight. He would call this evening when he returned to his home. He wouldn't want any interruptions. He took the paper out of his pocket while he walked to his car. Reading the name again, he thought of his own daughter. He couldn't imagine what a tough day this was for the mother. He tucked the paper back into his breast pocket as he unlocked the car door. It felt good to be doing something again. Joe could finally feel his pulse; he had been off the job for too long.

Joe is employed by ARD Investigations. He operated adequately as an investigator when he was not being thrown down staircases. At this time, he was still on medical leave due to his own imprudence. He had been working on a surveillance case for a very wealthy woman named Mrs. Rutledge, which involved cheating on her younger husband's part. It was a classic case of a man who loved his wife's money more than he loved his wife. Mrs. Rutledge wanted to expose the "two-timing bastard," as she put it.

After trailing the man on a few occasions, Joe had found himself sitting in a bar one rainy March evening, surveying his quarry. After a long forty minutes and a few drinks, the man, Douglas, had received a phone call after which he hurriedly stood up and left. Joe bolted out of his chair to follow on his coattails. The drink hit Joe instantly, the few he'd had while he sat in wait. Always one too many, that was Joe.

It had been raining harder and visibility was poor due to the settling fog. At some point Joe must have gotten their paths crossed as he followed the man past the office building down to the corner. Douglas abruptly crossed the street, a move Joe had not anticipated. He darted into the intersection just as the light was changing. Joe had cursed as he also stepped off the curb and into the pedestrian walkway, which by now was full of people. For a split second he thought he lost his target but then spotted him ahead veering off to the left. He hurried to catch up.

He followed a man, no longer Douglas, into a covered carpark. The man, who Joe believed to be Douglas, was heading to the staircase to the upper level. Joe wasn't planning on continuing up the steps, thinking it would look too obvious, but another man had come up behind him and with a shove had told him to keep walking. Joe had reluctantly walked on. Then on the staircase at the second level, Joe tried to make a run for it but was grabbed by the throat. He was slammed into a beam and stabbed. He looked down to where the knife had penetrated just as he was knocked backwards down the stairs.

He lay there helpless as a witness kindly called 999. He closed his eyes and softly moaned. He wasn't moaning because he was lying there, with people staring down at him in some sort of curious pity. He was moaning because Mr. Rutledge was likely in the arms of his lover by then, safe and sound.

For his troubles, he suffered bruised ribs and a stab wound to the belly. His client Mrs. Rutledge was most understanding, telling him to take the time he needed to recover. His colleagues along with David at the Police Department said that Joe had interrupted a drug deal. "Likely the Russians," David had said, as there had been a spike in drug use in the area, which was now notorious for Russian dealers. Joe had taken four weeks off the job. He hated being injured; it made him feel incompetent and incapable of getting the job done.

Staying at home wasn't agreeing with Joe. His wounds were healing but not his frame of mind. Fortunately his mood began to improve once he had started venturing out again. His first stop had been a visit to the pub to watch a football match with Simon. He had tired of being homebound and was looking forward to seeing his mates. He stayed longer than he would have, as he was waiting for Simon. But his friend hadn't showed up. It was that evening, or rather the morning after, that Joe found the body.

CHAPTER 6

Leaving the police station, Joe was at last heading to the hotel to have a chat with Thomas. Surprisingly, he felt an optimistic enthusiasm about the visit. Grabbing the first parking spot he could find, he cut the ignition and jumped out of the car. He walked the rest of the way to the Nether Edge, happy to be stretching his legs. Joe entered the building by the main hotel door rather than the pub entrance, hoping to find the innkeeper. Fortunately, Thomas was there, leaning in the doorway with his eyes on the television set hanging on the wall. He turned when he heard Joe enter. Thomas was a disheveled man about Joe's age and a bit taller. He wore khakis and suspenders over a well-worn checkered shirt.

Joe introduced himself and thanked the man for speaking to him. Thomas had no objection and ushered him into his dingy flat, which consisted of two rooms at the back of the reception area. Realizing he would not be invited to sit, Joe began questioning the man. He planned to keep it brief.

Thomas said Rita had worked for him for most of the past year. She usually didn't go too far from the hotel, so he found it odd when she hadn't shown up for work.

"I knocked on her door and I got no answer, tried every day, few times a day and on day four I figured something was wrong," he said as he rubbed the stubble on his chin.

"So you say she's been here less than a year?"

"Aye, only since she moved down from Barnsley. She answered an advertisement I placed for a chambermaid. I got a call from the proprietor there, saying they had a girl that wanted to take the job. She had been working for them at the Upton Arms for the past few years. The man said she'd had a bad run-in with a boyfriend so she was looking to move somewhere new. That's why he called me with a recommendation." Thomas shifted uneasily. "I wasn't going to report her being missing. My first thought was that she'd gone back to Barnsley."

"Why do you think she would do that, Thomas?"

"Maybe to see her old boyfriend? I'd heard he was a bit of a troublemaker who was not good to her. Having said that, I know she had not been seeing him as she had nawt good to say about him. But when she disappeared I thought maybe she went back."

"So, what made you realize she wasn't there after all?"

"I think it just didn't make sense to me. She had a job here and all. So, I called up there and spoke to someone who answered the phone. They remembered Rita and said she weren't there and besides, the boyfriend was long gone, moved away. And then I realized her bike was gone. If she were off somewhere on a bus she would have left her bike here." Thomas scratched his stubble again. "She were a lovely girl, just not very bright if you know what I mean. You could tell she'd had plenty of troubles." Thomas' expression changed slightly as he asked, "So did you really find her?"

"Yes, I did find her, I'm afraid."

"Could it be someone else and they got it wrong?"

"No, I can tell you she was identified. We are contacting family right now to have it officially confirmed." Joe noticed the man seemed agitated. "The police will let you know in due time, Thomas. Can I ask you if she had any friends who came around? Maybe she had a different boyfriend or maybe a girlfriend? Someone we could talk to?"

"She was always alone from what I saw. But she always kept busy. She even had a new job down at the local grocery store, stocking the shelves. That's why it didn't make sense she'd go anywhere."

"Which grocery store was that, Thomas?"

"It was at the Co-op store over on Banner Cross. She rode her bike over, since it wasn't too far. They hired her for evenings. She said it was to keep her apart from customers as she were always muttering. She said she didn't know she was doing it. But to me it were like she wasn't right in the head." With a glassy sheen in his eyes he added, "Do you think they'll find out what happened to 'er?"

"I hope so, Thomas, I know the police are looking into it and I'm sure you will hear from them once they have any news." Raising his finger in the air, he asked Thomas, "Just one last question. Do you know anyone around here who would hurt Rita? For any reason?"

Thomas shook his head violently. "No, I don't. Coppers already asked me that. Why is everyone asking me? How the hell would I know?"

There was something sinister about the man, but Joe couldn't quite put his finger on it. He seemed to know more than he was saying. Joe didn't believe he had killed Rita, but he had the suspicion that he was holding something back. He might need to come back to Thomas at a later date.

Joe walked out into the sunlight and got into his car, contemplating his next move. Pulling out onto the road, he told himself it was about time he made an appearance at ARD Investigations. As he drove along Abbeydale Road, he slowed the car, eyeing the pedestrians carefully. There was always the chance he might spot the bugger who stuck the knife in his belly. This was something Joe hadn't done in a while, but he told himself he would try more often, whenever the opportunity arose. Although a long shot, the guy must be out there somewhere. Driving to Abbey Lane just past the Millhouses, he then turned around and slowly drove back before turning in to his office building.

He arrived at his office with no luck at spotting the miscreant. Joe parked the car in his usual spot and walked through the front door with some trepidation. He was relieved that the lads were not mocking but more sympathetic about his misadventure. The botched surveillance was weighing heavily on him and although it was atypical behaviour, he felt awkward showing his face after his seven-week absence. But his timing was good as the office wasn't full of people. Less faces to deal with all at once. Those present were careful not to mock him or rub him the wrong way.

Except for Barry who came up with, "If you had have fallen onto an upholstery machine you'd be fully re-covered by now," which caused everyone to break out in laughter. Barry had provided the necessary icebreaker. Within minutes the atmosphere had settled to the usual banter and Joe felt a weight had been lifted off his shoulders. As it was late afternoon he and a few of his colleagues walked down the street to grab a pint at the local pub.

CHAPTER 7

Joe made himself a cup of tea as he eyed the slip of paper lying by the phone. Although anxious to be calling Mrs. Nowak he was preparing himself for how the woman would sound. It had been a few days since she had been informed of the death of her daughter. He hoped she was in a better emotional state than she had been when she first heard the news. Once settled, he picked up the phone and dialed the number.

The heavily accented woman picked up on the second ring. He introduced himself and expressed his deepest condolences. She thanked him for his kindness and talked for a long time, telling him things about the family. She spoke in a calm and subdued voice, perhaps in a state of shock.

Mrs. Nowak said that Rita had a brother, Stefan. Rita had left home when she was just fifteen years old and her brother was also fifteen. When grilled by his parents, Stefan had said he knew nothing of her leaving. Mrs. Nowak had never known whether or not to believe him. For years, she cried for Rita, so young. What horrors could have happened to her? She began retelling the story from the day her daughter ran away and the circumstances surrounding it. Mrs. Nowak explained that her husband was a hard man and had been physically abusive to her and the children.

"I've been tormented all these years, knowing I was weak and had failed miserably at protecting my children. And I have to admit that I did suspect my husband had forced himself onto my Rita. What could I do? I will never forgive myself for not speaking up for her. Now I think about it, I would have rather taken another beating than let him touch her one more time. I should have taken her to live with my sister." She whimpered softly before continuing, "I will forever feel the anguish of not being able to tell Rita how sorry I am."

Joe decided not to mention the fact that Rita had given birth to a child. Not now, not over the phone. He would need to do a detailed timeline to establish if there was a possibility that Rita's child belonged to her father.

"You mentioned Stefan was also fifteen when Rita ran away. Were they twins?" Joe was curious to know why the woman mentioned they were the same age but not said they were twins.

"No, not twins. Rita was born in January and Stefan in November of the same year. They are eleven months apart."

Joe had never heard of that before, of two siblings being born so close together. "What can you tell me about your son, Mrs. Nowak?"

"My Stefan will be twenty-four this year. He has been gone for nearly three years already, hard to believe. He hasn't been the same since Rita disappeared and had always told me he couldn't wait to leave home. It upset me to hear him talk like that. But the boy is smart. He is the smart one in the family; his mind was, you know, curious. The boy wanted to learn everything. He was always studying while holding more than one job. Stefan was saving his money, waiting for the day that he could leave."

Joe could hear her voice breaking up and gave her a minute to compose herself.

"Stefan grew up quickly after Rita left. He was a boy with big dreams, big ambitions. He finished school with a love of working with iron. I think it helped him. He could release a lot of anger and frustration in hammering and bending. And he had been lucky to have work as an apprentice in blacksmithing through a local business. Stefan had very supportive teachers who helped him along his way. Then he found an opportunity to move to Leicester to share a business there."

"Would you allow me to speak to your son? He may have spoken to Rita at some point over the years. Maybe he was keeping her secret. He might not want to speak to me but I'd like to try."

"Yes, he might want to talk to someone. Just not to me. He hated his father and blamed him for Rita leaving. He blamed me too. His father left shortly afterwards and we don't know if he was leaving us or if he went to look for Rita. Either way, Stefan has not had a man to speak to about these things. I have no way of knowing if he needs to talk about it or would prefer not to. But please do try."

"Has the coroner been in touch? He will need someone to come and identify the body, I'm sorry to tell you. It can be you or it can be your son."

"Yes we have been asked to come. I think my son will want to be the one to come. I am too far away and travel would not be easy for me. I'm not well, you see. And I don't know if I can see her like this."

Mrs. Nowak gave him Stefan's address and phone number in Leicester. Joe planned on asking Stefan if he would agree to see him when he took the eighty-minute drive into Sheffield to identify Rita.

"He works as a metal artist now." Joe realized that Mrs. Nowak was still talking. "He is trying to buy into the metalsmith shop where he works with the owner. The man is older and wants to retire soon so he's giving Stefan the opportunity to buy him out. He is very good at crafting kitchenware, chimes and wall hangings and the like. His shop is the busiest in the area."

Mrs. Nowak's pride was apparent. It must give her some real comfort to know that one of her children was doing well. The woman sounded heartbroken and in need of some consolation but while Joe was not unfeeling he was not prepared to get into a conversation about her life. Nor a discussion about Rita's death, for that matter. This was new territory for Joe, dealing with a dead body and the aftermath. Death had never been a big part of his job and he was still finding it unsettling. All he could see was Rita's eye on him. Perhaps she wanted him to get this done right.

CHAPTER 8

Joe sat in quiet thought. It was Wednesday morning and he had risen earlier than usual. He was now settled in his living room with his morning cup of coffee. The television was on but he wasn't listening. He was preoccupied instead with the beams of sunlight coming through the slits in the window blinds, mesmerized with the motes dancing in the rays. After a time, he stirred. The minutes had melted into an hour. Now he felt ready to call Stefan. He wondered if this would be an easy call for either of them.

The phone was answered with a deep, full-toned "Hullo, Stefan here."

The conversation was good and it put Joe at ease. Stefan felt most ready to come to Sheffield and had made arrangements with the coroner's office to come to identify his sister's body and look after funeral arrangements.

"I am hoping I can get some answers, find out what happened to her and maybe find out where she has been all this time. Do you think the police have some answers for me?"

"I don't think they know much more than me at this point, and I'm not sure how much they will be able to find out."

"Or you mean don't know how much time they will dedicate to finding out. Did you just tell me you were a PI? So, may I ask on whose behalf are you calling me? What I mean is, who are you working for?"

"I'm not working for anyone. This is personal. I found her, you see, lying there near my car. And I want to help if I can. I'd like it if I could talk to you when you are here. Would you be interested in meeting with me?"

"I would like that, yes. I am driving up in the morning. I'll hang a sign on the shop and be there by ten. Where will I see you?"

"What time are you seeing the police?"

"I'm meeting them at ten thirty, at the morgue on Watery Street, near the River Don."

"I'll be there as well," Joe promised.

"Thank you. Oddly it will make it easier if you are there. My mother pegged you as a good man."

Joe hung up the phone. Young Mr. Nowak sounded like a decent chap, bright and forthcoming.

Later that same day Joe was sitting in his office at ARD Investigations, deep in thought about Rita. She did have a criminal file but not because of the four years she had been involved in prostitution. Her criminal record had stemmed from an incident where she had broken into a beauty salon, looking for a dry place to sleep. While there, she had taken money, possibly for her drug habit. The girl had been arrested while exiting the building; someone having alerted the police. Joe thought it unlikely she was killed for that reason, as that was quite a few years ago.

Why would a young girl barely seventeen, turn to prostitution? Records revealed nothing beyond that. And there was no indication that she was currently engaging in any prostitution or drug use. But what was she doing in the Fulwood area, on Joe's street? Lying beside his car?

The shrill ring of the phone made him jump.

"Good morning, Mr. Parrott? This is Marion Rutledge."

Mrs. Rutledge was his client for whom he took his graceless plunge down the staircase of a building while following the wayward bastard, Douglas Rutledge.

Feeling a twinge of his embarrassment return, he greeted her warmly.

"And a pleasant morning to you as well, Mrs. Rutledge."

"I am happy to hear that you are back at work and that you are recovering. I had a real fright."

"It certainly didn't go as I had planned, ma'am. I have no idea how I lost sight of him. Problem is, everyone seems to wear black these days so I plead innocent on the confusion. I just wish I knew who I did follow into the parkade. And why he stabbed me. But I am ready to get back on it, if you need me. I haven't yet got you what you are paying for."

Mrs. Rutledge paused briefly before answering. "Actually, that's why I am calling. My husband is leaving me, Mr. Parrott. He says he's happy to be broke, he doesn't want anything from me." He heard the woman laugh lightly. "I somehow feel liberated, you know? In a sense, this makes everything so much easier for me. And it spares me further embarrassment of resorting to having him followed."

Mrs. Rutledge was likely in her sixties. She was very old school English. Everything needed to be proper, from her grooming right down to her posh, blathering speech, which sounded almost forced. She talked through her teeth, her lips barely moving. All her words were running into one long exasperating statement. Joe very nearly felt an affinity towards the husband for leaving.

"I don't know whether to say sorry or congratulations, ma'am. Is this a travesty or a blessing?"

"Quite the latter, my dear Mr. Parrott. When you think about it, I had been reduced to hiring a private eye. It obviously was not a good marriage, and this is likely the best way it could end. Are you married, Mr. Parrott?"

"I was married once, but it ended. She has recently re-married."

"Well, we have that in common then, don't we? So with that said, might I ask that you send your final bill so I can settle up with you? I can't thank you enough, and again I am sorry you were stabbed, seems like now it was all for nothing."

"Will do, Mrs. Rutledge. Cheers." Joe found it very unlikely they had anything in common. He also didn't find her last remark very inspirational, and perhaps a little unnecessary. Was she taking the mickey? Joe hung up the phone sharply. Sometimes he wondered how good he was at his job.

CHAPTER 9

Joe was forty-four years old and perhaps it was too late to be asking this question. An only child, he had lost all friends at an early age when his father emigrated from Seattle. At the age of eight he felt disoriented and alone at his new school, in this place where everyone talked strangely. He had been grateful for Simon's friendship but they weren't exactly shining examples of ambition. They finished school together, taking a gap year but ended up doing nothing with it.

They had broadened that gap and did nothing for the following year as well. Simon, lanky and boyish, loved the ladies but they didn't love him back. He grew up to be an awkward, perpetually horny nerd who never quite learned how to talk to girls. He could never seem to find the balance between complimentary and crude. While not exactly repulsive, he had a tendency to be crudely unpleasant.

Joe on the other hand had no such problems. He enjoyed a good shag and never needed to ask for it. He wasn't a tall man, about five foot eleven if he stood at attention but he was what the girls would consider a hunk. He had a slim but solid frame and was oozing with testosterone, exuding charm and strength. He was polite and quiet, with an easy-going manner and extremely approachable. Unlike Simon, Joe wasn't big on conversation, choosing to be more of a bystander, and the girls seemed drawn to his reserve.

Graduating with no apparent focus, they spent their afternoons kicking a soccer ball around at Endcliffe Park waiting for their mates to finish classes or work. They had become accustomed to sleeping until eleven. Evenings were spent at the pub playing darts or cribbage. They would drive home late at night, the CD playing Pink Floyd's "The Wall" at top volume. During that period, Joe's only responsibility would be helping his dad at the sheep farm, particularly during lambing, or with any heavy lifting.

The two eventually found employment with the help of Simon's uncle, who was in an upper management position at CORP Safety and Protection. Neither had any experience or training with security and were offered entry-level positions. Joe took a posting in the department of events and gatherings, in crowd and safety control, while Simon opted for a posting to work as a manned guard, occasionally taking short turns in key holding services and answering alarms and such.

The girl that caught Simon's eye worked at CORP as well, in the reception area. She met him on the first day when they went for their interview with Simon's uncle. She smiled at Simon and introduced herself as Eva Fisher. Nearly a year later she asked him out, saying she gave up waiting for him to ask her. Within a year, they were married.

It was a good marriage until she started to feel that he was no longer interested in her. Her girlfriends disliked the way he stared into their blouses instead of their faces. Eva said she had once overheard him speaking to one of her friends while they were leaving a party. Simon was drunk, and he had leaned over and asked her to "show him her pink bits." He later said it was bollocks, but nonetheless, Eva packed up and left. Joe was aware that there are always two sides to every story, and that a lot can go on behind closed doors. Frankly, he just didn't want to know. He was aware of Simon's bad habits.

Simon was like a brother, never a day that they weren't in touch. He relied heavily on Joe for comfort during the separation process but when Eva finally moved out, he withdrew for a spell. Because of Simon's inability to deal with obstacles of any sort, this came as a real blow to him. He had considered himself blessed when she had fallen in love with him. Now he was only thirty-seven and he thought his life was over.

It was actually a bit frightening how he was behaving during that period. When drinking he could become loud and obnoxious. Joe didn't push to be with him and he felt relieved and somewhat grateful for the opportunity to distance himself from the drama. But eventually Simon had bounced back.

A couple of years after Simon was married, Joe met Janet. He had been standing on a street corner, waiting for the light to change, when she sprinted past him yelling "bollocks" just as the bus was pulling away. Before she could stop, she somehow stumbled. In one grandiose movement her shoe slipped from her foot, spiraling through the air and landing at Joe's feet. He bent to pick it up as she hobbled back towards him, her face exploding into a magnificent grin. If there could be romance in losing one's shoe, Joe had found it.

She had charm and Joe was rightly affected by it. Things began to swiftly change. He felt a purpose for the first time in his life. Joe had woken up. It was only then, with Janet, that he felt a belonging and had a new appetite for what the world had to offer. He left CORP shortly afterwards and started his career as a private investigator, helping to pay for Janet's training as a Band 5 nurse and beyond a Band 7 level.

But over the following years, as he strived to be good at his job, it was becoming increasingly obvious that he was not good at marriage. Although it was agreeable while it lasted, the travesty was that it didn't last. Their happiness morphed into discord, held together only by their daughter, Susan. Eventually, they both wanted out.

So when it was Joe's turn to divorce, it was much the opposite scenario from Simon. It was quiet and civilized, in part because their daughter was now seventeen. More importantly because that's just the kind of people they were. He helped Janet move to Manchester where she had a job waiting. Her father had been good to them but had a penchant for being overbearing. He was the one who had convinced them it was time to start a family. He gifted them a house with his sweepstakes winning because he wanted them to have a good home for his many grandchildren.

Grandchildren had turned into only one granddaughter. Their plans didn't allow for more because of personal goals and disagreements about who would mind the baby and whose priorities were most important. Both were career-minded people who didn't put enough thought into the responsibilities of having children.

Joe slowed his drinking after Janet left. He and Simon had become serious drinkers. It had been the pub nights with Simon after his divorce from Eva when things got really bad. Joe likely gave too much attention to Simon's situation rather than watching his own. With the failure of the marriage came the freedom for carousal.

But aside from the parenting problems and the lousy hours of the job, the drinking was the final straw and ultimately pushed Janet to divorce. Only after he was alone did he realize how badly he needed to clean up his act with alcohol, drinking considerably less now.

Life had slowed down to a nice rhythm. Gone were the late pub nights where he couldn't remember getting home. No more a lot of things. Reflecting back, he realized that he had been living as someone else. Joe hated to admit it, but he couldn't remember the last time he kicked a soccer ball around. Or the last time he totally disappeared into the arms of a bewitchingly captivating woman.

His life now consists of time with Susan, spying on husbands, tracking down law breakers, and his most often one-pint limit at the end of his day, which was usually taken at Fox House with Carole serving.

CHAPTER 10

Stefan Nowak arrived the following morning, having closed his shop early for the day as promised. Joe had arranged to meet him and DI Harry Wilkes downtown near the mortuary. Somehow he had no problem recognizing the fair-haired young man that was walking with purpose towards him. Stefan was as tall as Joe but slight. He had long straight white-blonde hair and wispy whiskers. Joe thought him to be a good-looking young man. After a somber hello and a handshake, Joe followed the DI and a very nervous Stefan down the staircase to see Rita. Ganesh escorted the men into the cold, dimly lit room. It was the first time Joe had seen the body since it was cleaned up.

Rita was laid on a cot, covered with a white sheet to her neck, only her hand visible. She now looked human as opposed to the bloody corpse in the lane. Joe was grateful for the opportunity to humanize Rita, to see her as a real girl, although now heavily made up. He noticed how much she and Stefan looked alike. He had the same translucent skin, like tissue paper, blue veined and pale. It was hard to

49

tell if she shared his high cheekbones and white-blonde hair, the look of repression in his eyes likely ingrained from a childhood of abuse. Joe felt compassion for Stefan, as he so wanted his sister to be alive.

Stefan cautiously approached the table, walking around the side to peer directly at the small face. Watching him was heart-rending. His legs seemed to give out as he tried to take a step forward and his hand shook as he reached out to stroke her hair. Grabbing the side of the gurney for support, his lip quivering uncontrollably, Stefan reached over and gently took his sister's hand in his. He stood there for a few moments, whispering inaudibly as he said goodbye to his sister. When he was ready, he looked up at Ganesh and nodded, and Ganesh came over and pulled the sheet up over her face.

Ganesh and the DI took the young man into the office to complete the documents. Joe waited in the lobby. Once Stefan had concluded his business he walked out to Joe with a look that indicated he was ready to leave. Saying goodbye to Ganesh and Wilkes, the two of them walked outside. They stood on the street corner, Joe waiting for Stefan to make the first move. After a few moments the young man spoke.

"Wow, that was tough. I know I haven't seen my sister in what seems like forever. Maybe nine years? It feels like I've never known her, we were so young. But coming here and seeing her…" He shifted to his other foot and crossed his arms across his chest. "What I mean is, saying goodbye here, in this way, brings on some pretty powerful emotions." He ran his fingers across his wispy beard and continued.

"That man said that Rita likely had a baby. So does she have a child somewhere?"

"I don't know that. We only know that she had definitely given birth to one. But no one came forward to report her missing on behalf of a child, so we don't know if there is one."

"What could have happened to the baby?"

"I have no idea. I don't think it's being investigated, only her murder is. I don't know if the child even lived."

"If there is any way to find out? I mean, can you help me? Will you help me? I don't know if the killer will be caught, but if we can find the child, it will keep a big part of her alive."

"Stefan, I'm sure the police will do their best to find the killer."

"Can you help find the killer?"

"Well, I can try but the key will be in finding some clue, any clue to what might have happened. I need to look into where she lived, who she knew, where she went."

"I want to hire you, Joe. I want to do everything I can to find out. And I can help you! I don't live that far away." He stood straight, his shoulders back in commanding fashion. He was serious.

Joe's answer was immediate. "This one's on me, and yes, I will help you.

"I can't let you do it for nothing."

"I still feel if I had found her in time I could have saved her. At least let me check into it on my own and see what I can come up with. Let's start with a bit of background on her. Can you help me there?"

"Let's go have a coffee and I'll tell you what I know. Come on, I'll buy." With deliberation, Stefan marched ahead until he at last turned around and asked Joe, "Is there a coffee shop around here somewhere?"

Joe smiled to himself and, turning Stefan around, headed him in the other direction.

Over a steaming mug of tea, Stefan filled Joe in on the little he knew about his sister. He had such a short time with her.

"I didn't really know her, when I think back. She was independent as hell, never wanted help with anything. And she was always withdrawn, private. We were too different to be close. I remember running after her on the way to school. I was always yelling for her to wait up, but she walked fast so as not to walk with me. Did you know we are practically twins? She always said we were twins but I was late for the party and she was tired of always waiting for me."

Stefan painted a tragic picture of affliction and abuse. According to him, Dad beat up Mom, and Rita as well.

"I got cuffed around the head for sure, but he really let loose on Mum and Rita. My mum was a cleaning lady, you see. She had a job cleaning the estate apartments where we lived. My dad started accusing her of sleeping with the men who lived in the other apartments. He was bonkers. I don't know why she took it, and it just got worse and worse."

Stefan went on to tell him about a woman Sadie who worked at the corner store. "She recollected when Mum was too bruised up to go out in public she would send me and Rita with a shopping list. This Sadie would share these stories with me whenever I went into the store, even years after Rita had left. I thought it was harsh, the way she'd always rub that in, especially since I was so young. She were a real cow. I didn't need to be hearing it all the time."

Stefan leaned back in his chair. "I mean, I can't say I blame Rita for leaving. We had a shit life. Even after Dad left, I realized my mum was a terrible mother. I learned later how different it was for us, from how my school friends had it. We didn't laugh much. I don't remember being hugged. There was no sitting around the table for meals, talking about our day like they do on TV. It were always quiet, and tense, and we were told not to move, not to talk. It was only when I was older and I watched movies like Back to the Future and ET that I realized our family weren't normal. I think me mum and dad were both selfish. It would have been better if they'd given us away."

Joe took a handful of peanuts and a healthy swig of his beer as Stefan took a slow sip of his tea. "Then there were the hints that Dad was sexually abusing Rita. The neighbours told me this, can you believe it? I was young and didn't understand these things. There were telltale signs, people said. It made me sick to think it."

"What kind of signs?" Joe asked.

"They said she had become secretive and she was not attending school any more. She seemed to be afraid of Dad and of Mum, like she couldn't trust Mum to protect her. And she stopped talking to me. When she ran away Mum was inconsolable and Dad was furious. He took it out on Mum, blaming her for letting Rita go. At that point it was dangerous for either of us to try to leave. I was thinking that maybe Rita did the right thing and I should go too, but then Dad left."

Joe sat forward, his arms resting on the table. "I will help you, Stefan, like I said. But I can't promise what I might or might not find, as long as you know that."

Checking the time before standing up, Stefan smiled and offered Joe his hand. "That's about good enough for me, Mr. Parrott. Thank you. It's getting late and I need to get back and pick up the paperwork for Rita's cremation before I head home."

Saying goodbye to Stefan, Joe agreed they would talk soon. By early afternoon, Stefan was on his way back to Leicester and Joe went about his day. He drove straight back to his office and busied himself with the stack of documents piled in his tray. He had a mess of paperwork to clear away from his desk and of course there was the Rutledge file to close.

Stopping in at Fox House on his way home, he had just greeted Carole and had barely opened his mouth for conversation when he heard a familiar squeak behind him. It was Simon, who was suddenly there, grabbing him by the scruff of his neck and laughing loudly.

Looking at Carole, he called out, "Give us a pint of Guinness please, will you? Thanks, love." Turning to Joe, he asked, "Where have you been, then?"

"I've been asking you the same thing. I've rung you a few times."

"I've been working. It's been busy, you know? And I have these new issues at home. Liz is moving in slowly. She's doing it transitional like, to make it easier on her daughter. Seems a strange thing me to have so much fuss about getting on with your life. Her kid should do the same. This is bullshit."

Joe shook his head at the lack of eloquence of his friend. "I told you before, Simon, it's delicate with kids."

Still, Joe felt good to be here catching up with Simon He spent over an hour before heading on his way. He felt all of the muscles in his neck and jaw relax as they fell into their banter. Carole walked over to be with them as often as she could, between customers, but Simon was so engrossed in conversation that she would leave again without contributing a word. Joe was helplessly aware that he had very little opportunity for any dialogue with her today, but she smiled at him and nodded knowingly. He winked back in appreciation.

.

CHAPTER 11

Joe left the house early, setting off on foot. He needed a brisk walk to clear his head before getting into his car. There were days like today when he felt he needed to find a new place to park his car. The memory of Rita would come back to him whenever he approached the spot, that haunting look of her eye on him. He found it acutely disturbing. After twenty minutes, he slowed his pace, then turned to head back home. It was time to start his day.

Now officially on the job, his first objective was to find out about Rita's past and about the child. Tracking Rita's movements wouldn't be easy, but with patience, he just might have success. He didn't know whether to start back and come forward in time or the other way around. To find out about the child he decided to go back to the beginning and work forward. He started at the Register Offices, but he was unable to find any information. There was no record of anyone named Rita Nowak.

The earliest record Joe could find of Rita was that she had been living in a homeless shelter in a northern part

of Sheffield. Joe decided to pop in at the shelter the following day, once mid-morning traffic had subsided. He
found parking directly in front of the nondescript building.
Climbing the steps and straightening his tie, he rang the
doorbell. Once he explained who he was, they invited him
in, suddenly eager to speak with him.

After having a word with a few of the employees he was
led to a waiting room, where he was invited to sit down. He
took a seat on an old faded green couch. It looked drab in
an otherwise cheerful room. A big urn of yellow and red silk
flowers was standing a few feet away in an effort to bring
some colour to the sofa. A beautiful tapestry hung on the
wall, possibly Spanish or Portuguese based on the patterns.
Overhead, the chandelier gleamed. A stack of cooking
magazines sat on the small circular table directly in front of
the sofa.

After what seemed a very long wait, a woman quickly
entered the room. Offering her hand, she introduced herself
as June. She looked to be in her early seventies, with blue-
grey hair wound in a long thick braid. Her cheeks shone as
if freshly scrubbed and the hazel twinkled inside her sparkling eyes. Joe thought of Mrs. Clause, if there was one. Her
expressions suggested she was a kind woman.

June sat down in the chair nearest to him, their knees
almost touching. After Joe explained to her what information he was looking for, June sat back, a regretful look on
her face. June didn't remember Rita but did speculate she
knew someone who might.

"I'm sorry, but we have so many girls come through
these doors, and I can no longer keep track of them beyond

a few years. But we had a counsellor here, Aisha Hunt, who could very well remember the girl. Back then Mrs. Hunt worked closely with most of them. I just might know where she now works, and I would be happy to make inquiries."

"May I ask, how did Rita slip through the cracks? She was so young. Does that not seem unusual to you? Did no one try hard enough to find her on the missing persons database?"

She smiled kindly. "It's almost impossible to keep track of them all, Mr. Parrott. And the circumstances vary greatly. Most homeless are not runaways so we don't check each one to see if that's the case. Our project workers are mostly concerned with immediate needs."

"I wonder if anyone knew she was pregnant when she arrived. I'm curious what the circumstances were surrounding that. For example, did she have a man in her life or maybe she was raped?"

"Homeless young women often search for someone to love and protect them and she may have become sexually active either as a victim of rape, like you say, or as a way to get a man to avoid being alone. They will cling to it even if the relationship is a bad one. Many of them, as many as half, are or have been pregnant. I will track down Mrs. Hunt and ask her if she'd be willing to speak to you. So how can I get in touch with you?"

"I appreciate your help more than you know, June," Joe said as he stood to leave. He pulled his wallet out of the back pocket of his chinos and handed her his card with both his numbers. "I can be reached any time, but I'm not pressuring you. I hope you know that."

June shook her head. "I don't feel at all pressured and I don't anticipate this will take very long. Goodbye, Mr. Parrott, it was lovely to meet you."

Joe walked back to his car, grateful for this tidbit of information to get him started.

Later that afternoon he called Stefan from his office. The lad sounded very pleased with this news.

"I will let you know if June makes contact and more importantly, if this person remembers anything and will agree to speak with us. I don't know if it will take a day or a week, but I will call you the second I hear anything," was Joe's effort to keep Stefan from driving up right away.

Two days later, there was good news. June called to say that the social worker Aisha was still local. Mrs. Hunt now works for Women's Aid, running a housing and refuge for young women and their children. Hanging up from June, Joe called the number that she gave him. Disappointed to hear a voice on an answering machine, he debated hanging up and trying later. He changed his mind last minute and left his message.

It was getting late and Joe realized he hadn't eaten much since noon. He had just opened the refrigerator door when his phone rang. It was Mrs. Hunt returning his call. She was extremely sorry to hear about Rita, and she was more than willing to have a chat.

"I remember her well. I'd like to believe that for a time we were quite close and had formed a bond. She had learned to trust me. But just so you know, it wasn't until after she had her baby that she told me her name was Rita. She had led us to believe her name was Stephanie. This would be the reason why you've found no record of her, and perhaps why June didn't remember her."

Joe thought about this. Stephanie would be the feminine of her brother's name. It would be her way of being anonymous, to avoid detection. "She has a brother named Stefan. That could be where she got the name from."

"Yes, that could be very likely the case."

"I hope you don't mind but Stefan would like to join me when I visit you."

"Please do bring him. I would very much like to meet her brother," was her reply.

The plan was to meet on a day convenient to Mrs. Hunt's schedule, and so it was decided the two men would come to the shelter on the following Wednesday, at the end of her shift. Joe hung up the phone feeling satisfied. He had accomplished something big today.

It was midday, and Joe was leaving the house in a hurry. While walking to the rear of the car to put some things into the boot, something suddenly dawned on him. Thomas at the Nether Edge told him that Rita went everywhere on her bike. Why had he not remembered that? So where was her bike? He would need to call DI Wilkes to see if a bike was found when they were searching the area around the body.

Otherwise, he would ask Thomas if the bike was possibly still at the hotel, although Joe was sure he said it was not there. He would also need to check at the Co-op as there was the possibility Rita had left it at work. Finding it may not reveal anything but it was a big question as to its whereabouts.

While it was out of his way, he decided to drive to the police station. He eventually found David, who also didn't recall anything about a bike. Joe related what Thomas had told him.

"Did Thomas hold this information back from police? Or did they not ask the right questions?" thought Joe aloud.

"Maybe he didn't think of it at the time. Not everything is important to everyone at any given moment. Maybe he was focusing on the fact that she was dead?" offered David as he headed towards the stack of case files in the next room. Walking back to where Joe was waiting, his eyes glued to an open file he was carrying, he confirmed that there was no bike listed in the items recovered from the scene.

"I'll speak to DI Wilkes about it. They may need to go back again, but right now I couldn't say when that might happen. It is, after all, only a bike," was David's last comment.

Joe thanked David but, to himself, decided he'd do his own search in the morning. It could be important.

CHAPTER 12

Joe walked slowly down the corridor at the morgue. His footsteps echoed in the empty hallway, adding an eerie feeling to the emptiness. The shine from the waxed linoleum floors reflected the glaring fluorescent lights from overhead. His legs were shaking as he reached the end of the hallway and headed down the stairs. Ganesh, in his green scrubs, led him into the room where a figure cloaked in a white sheet lay on the gurney ahead. He inched his way towards the body, noticing the sheet was pulled away from the face. Bending over he broke into a sweat. Susan was lying there before him. Gripped by terror he felt himself collapsing. He wanted to run. The scream reverberated through the room. The image slowly disappeared into fragments as he began to come to.

Joe sat upright, now fully awake. His heart was pounding. The bed sheets were wet from perspiration. Joe got up to get a glass of cold water. He looked at the clock. It was three in the morning. It had been a long time since he had a bad dream. Keeping the covers well off his face, he was soon asleep.

He woke late and was happy to lay for awhile listening to the sounds of the outdoors coming through his open window. These were soothing sounds; the wood pigeons, the bleating of the lambs, a dog barking somewhere in the distance.

Despite the nightmare, Joe felt healthy today. His knife wound had healed completely and his ribs felt much better. The doctor had said he was very fortunate the knife had not penetrated or severed any major organs. Nothing a few internal stitches couldn't fix. He had been a bit concerned with the lifting and twisting with the hay bales but he felt no after effects.

Turning on the television to distract his thoughts, he had a shower and eventually went outside to put out the trash bin. This morning, he planned to do a search of the area to see if he could spot Rita's bike, which seemed to have temporarily disappeared. As Joe walked down his front steps, he ran into his neighbour Rob, who was standing not far from the spot where Rita's body was found. He cursed himself for not seeing him sooner so he could have avoided him.

Rob was an average-looking man but not average otherwise. He was long ago retired from his position as a schoolteacher, having resigned well ahead of schedule due to bad nerves. Years of taunting by his students had taken its toll; he had never learned how to handle them. This resulted in a nervous breakdown. He had once told Joe that he was fundamentally weak and ordinary, and he had failed to inspire anyone. Rob was not a bad man just not a noticeable one. Even his tiresome, colourless morning greetings annoyed Joe.

It's not that Joe disliked the man, he just felt he had nothing to say to him. He had tried for conversation over the years, inviting Rob for a pint or to watch a game at the pub but his attempts were unsuccessful. Rob had shook his head and strongly declined, saying it was not for him. But today, with a big smile, Joe said good morning to his neighbor. Rob muttered a hello in response. And so with a congenial smile and a slap on the shoulder Joe was on his way, not giving the man time to say anything further.

Joe carried on his search, not quite knowing in which direction to look. He slowly made his way towards Whitely Woods Trail and carried along Porter Brook. Beneath his feet lay a soft bed of mulched flora, dulling his footsteps. At this point he figured he had gone too far, as anyone wanting to hide a bike would likely not come this far out of the way. He would try another direction on another day.

It was a still, misty morning and Joe felt like turning this into a bit of a hike. He loved mornings like this, so he decided to carry on to the round house before turning back. The sound of crunching gravel under his feet turned into that of swishing grass.

As he cut across the pastures he was welcomed by small clusters of sheep scattered across the fields. They all stopped their eating and raised their heads to stare at him as he walked by. Their blank, almost moronic faces made Joe want to laugh. He watched their mouths move with the omnipresent sound of their bleating, in disharmonious chorus. Two brave young lambs started running towards him before stopping in their tracks and slowly turning away.

Joe's cell phone rang just as he was nearing home. He was surprised to hear that it was Stefan saying he was on his way into Sheffield. He wanted to help Joe look for the bike and would be there in less than an hour. Not having the heart to say he had just searched, he let Stefan come, knowing it would make him feel better to be assisting in some way. It looked like Joe would have his exercise today. He gave Stefan directions to where he lived.

It was the first time Stefan had been to where Joe lived. He wanted to see the location where Joe had found his sister, pausing only briefly to gaze at the spot. Fortunately, enough time had passed that there was no remaining trace of what had occurred there. Then he looked up at Joe saying, "Okay, so where should we begin?"

They conducted a search in the opposite direction of where Joe had been earlier. It turned into more of a hike and a chat. Stefan's demeanour was considerably different now. He seemed subdued and thoughtful. Joe watched him as he walked around, his head down checking the ground.

"Do you have anyone special, Joe?"

"Who, me? Not really. There's this woman, but she's more a mate than anything. I have my daughter and my job, mostly."

Stefan responded to this by saying, "I always felt I was doing okay, but suddenly I feel like I don't have anything. My life is actually a bit lonely right now, given the circumstances. Do you think I will always feel this way?" He looked over at Joe, who saw a new fragility in his soulful eyes.

"It's hard to say, Stefan. But I don't think those feelings will last forever. We adapt."

With nothing left to do after their search, Stefan announced he would be getting back.

"Want to come in for a beer?" offered Joe.

Stefan shook his head, "No, I really just came to pick up Rita's ashes, so I wanted to pop over and help you with this search. I'll be going now. I want to get back before traffic. Besides, I'll see you soon enough for the meeting with Mrs. Hunt, right?"

Joe watched as he got into his old blue Fiat and started the engine. Pulling out onto the roadway, Stefan looked in his rear-view mirror and gave him a wave.

CHAPTER 13

The next few days passed quickly. Before Joe knew it, he was sitting at his desk listening to the familiar voice in the foyer. Young Stefan had arrived for their meeting with Mrs. Hunt. After a tempered hello to those around him, Stefan and Joe were on their way. Stefan was seemingly and understandably nervous at getting this close to someone who had known his sister so well. Within ten minutes they arrived at the refuge. The building was not recognizable as a shelter which was likely intentional, the idea being to help these women remain anonymous in case anyone was looking for them.

They climbed the stairs and rang the doorbell. Within a few seconds, the door was opened. They were warmly greeted and instantly addressed by their names, which made Stefan's shoulders go down as he released some of his tension.

The woman introduced herself as Aisha Hunt. She was a stunningly attractive brunette, tall and slim, with dark brown eyes and a broad smile that rose slightly higher on one side, causing a dimple on her cheek. She wore no jewelry except for a thin gold chain with a small locket, which rested in the space below her collarbone. She was dressed smartly in a tailored dress that came just below the knee, and flat sandals.

Both men were silent as Mrs. Hunt led them down a corridor and into her office. Joe experienced an unmistakable feeling of calm in this woman's presence. Once seated and having offered the men tea or coffee, she settled into her chair.

Turning to Stefan with a look of recognition, she said, "You look very much like your sister. I am terribly sorry for your loss."

Stefan thanked her quietly; his body language indicated he had nothing further to say.

Turning then to Joe, Mrs. Hunt swept her hair back over her shoulder and asked, "So is Janet Parrott your wife?"

"Well that's a yes and no, I suppose. Yes, in that she was, and no, that she's not any longer."

"I could never forget a name like that, or the person, for that matter. Janet was a caring and competent person. She was working at the hospital when I brought Rita in. Actually I am sure that Janet had helped deliver the baby, as it was quite a tough birth."

Joe noticed how subtly and effectively she had avoided further talk about him no longer being married to Janet. He noticed an accent. Was it Italian? French? He couldn't quite make it out.

"It was a tragic story by all accounts. Rita didn't know she was pregnant until I had noticed the changes in her body. I took her to Royal Hallamshire Hospital, where it was determined she was already seven months gone. At the hospital she kept talking about some man. 'Her man', she would call him. She was saying that he was a cop and would come for her."

"Was she okay?" asked Stefan. "I mean, was she hurting or suffering or anything?"

Mrs. Hunt leaned forward in her chair and touching his arm warmly said, "I believe she was fine that way. She was just confused. And she kept repeating, 'He said he'd be back,' to which none of us knew quite how to respond."

Sitting back again, she continued, "We all thought she was making it up as she didn't even have a name for him. Either that or she was covering for someone who had done this to her, perhaps a boyfriend who ran, or someone older in a position of authority. The maternity nurse gave her a thorough check-up and then sent her back to the shelter."

"So did she lie about her age? She obviously didn't give her real name and she didn't have any ID. Did they not check her with missing persons?" Suddenly Stefan had a lot of questions.

"There would be many reasons why they didn't. She may have lied about her age, yes, or her circumstances. Perhaps they did try to trace Stephanie Nowak but would have come up empty-handed. It's impossible to keep track, and I hope it doesn't sound like I'm making excuses."

"Please go on, there's no fault here," said Joe encouragingly. He couldn't stop thinking of Susan. What if these things have happened to her? It made him realize how out of touch he was with things that went on in the city.

"She was brought back to hospital when she went into labour. Rita was frail and had a difficult delivery, and I believe it was your ex-wife who assisted in the emergency C-section. She stayed in hospital for three days before being released back to us. As she was young and homeless, the baby was taken away by social services. And inevitably the baby was put up for adoption. Rita at sixteen was a child herself and had since disappeared again, so decisions needed to be made on behalf of the child. He was such a wee boy."

Mrs. Hunt went on to tell them how Children and Adolescent services had visited Rita afterwards to discuss her own physical and mental wellbeing.

"By then, she told me her name was Rita and not Stephanie. I'm not sure what changed, why she wanted to tell me right then. She was becoming uncooperative, all the time crying for her baby. This was a very hard time for her, being so young, going through the pain of childbirth, frightened and perhaps not fully understanding everything that was happening. Then to be taken away from that child, still healing, her hormones raging, and strange people around her, taking control… There were subsequent follow-up appointments after she went back to shelter to finish healing. She cried and cried. She was angry with them all. We thought she had started to calm down but then one day she ran away."

She paused to offer some more tea before continuing. "Rita left the shelter shortly afterwards, and efforts to find her proved futile. I believe it was just over a year later, around Christmas, when I was driving north to visit family that I spotted Rita on the street. I pulled over, got out of the car, and ran towards her like an idiot, fearing I may lose her again.

It turns out she was squatting in the area of Kelham Island, relying on prostitution and it seemed pretty obvious that she was on drugs. I should say, it certainly seemed obvious to me. I knew her well enough to see that she was probably high. I think she remembered who I was. We spoke for a few brief moments before she turned and walked away. But after that I would visit her regularly, walk around the area until I found her.

I would say for about two years I visited her, even though the girl was so spaced out, I wasn't always sure she knew who I was. She would accept my help but only from a safe distance. Getting her anywhere safe would have been impossible. Still, she would sit and talk to me, each time for longer periods. I would bring her clothing and food, but never money. But after an arrest, one night in jail and being fingerprinted and having mug shots, she seemed ready to leave that life behind. So I slowly began bringing Rita back to the real world."

"You are an angel." Stefan seemed overwhelmed. "It seems you saved my sister more than once."

"I wish I could have done more, really, but it was at least something." She went on to say, "You see I am a social worker now, but I started out working as an adoption support officer within the agency. That's what led me to running this shelter. I hope I can help these homeless girls before they get themselves into trouble. But as is often the case, they arrive already with child. My desire was strong to help Rita in any way I could."

Mrs. Hunt told Joe and Stefan that with her help, Rita found a job at a small inn just north of Sheffield, in Barnsley. "This would have been about five years ago now, I think. In exchange for work they gave her a small room to call her own, at the back of the inn, and her meals. Although I stopped visiting Rita, the proprietor, Mr. Darwent was always willing to keep me up to date on the occasions that I called him. It was gradual, but she thrived and had stayed clean of drugs. I no longer have Mr. Darwent's number but I would imagine he's still there."

"It's easy enough for me to find out, Mrs. Hunt. I can Google it, or just ring them."

"Oh, please call me Aisha." The woman blushed slightly at Joe's formal use of her name.

"But we will leave you now, as you have given us a lot of your time and I believe your work day has ended."

Both men stood to make their leave, giving her a warm handshake, Stefan going so far as to hug the woman.

Aisha said good bye to them, and then to Joe she added, "Come back any time if you need any more information. I would be happy to help in any way I can."

As they made their way to where the cars were parked, Stefan broke the silence by saying, "I think she's nice."

"Aye, she looks a good woman."

"I feel better having met her. She was great to Rita. And she really helped her, don't you think?"

Joe put his arm on the boy's shoulder and said, "Aye, she did at that."

Stefan broke into a big smile as he looked over at Joe. "I think she fancies you."

"Give over," said Joe, with a startled look on his face. "Where would you get a silly idea like that? She's likely married. And besides, I'm too old for her."

"She's not that young, Joe."

"Well, a lot younger than me. And I'm not much in a courting mood these days."

"Oh, I get it, you old codger, you're an old man, are you? Where's your romance?"

"Just shut up and walk, Stefan." Joe was frowning.

"Bloody hell, Joe. Who peed in your pudding?"

CHAPTER 14

Joe needed a shave and a shower. He had become some-what consumed with this case in the past few days. He still could not figure out what Rita would have been doing in Fulwood. Even after pondering several scenarios, he could not come up with anything viable at this point. He admitted he still didn't know enough about Rita There were as yet no clues. He needed a decent meal and was not prepared to cook, so he headed off to his local pub for a good greasy meal, followed by an early night.

By morning, he felt renewed. It's amazing what a large meal, a long hot shower and a good sleep could do for someone. After spending most of the day at home, his next move was to visit the grocery store where Rita had recently become employed. Thomas had mentioned she had worked part time evenings stocking the shelves, so his plan was to show up early in the evening. It was far more likely that whoever would be there at that time of day would have known her.

Before leaving the house, he called Simon again but still no answer. The man had been somewhat unavailable these past few days. Joe dismissed it as being either busy at work or plans with Liz.

Parking outside of the Co-op, Joe noticed the parking lot was quite empty given the time of day. He walked into the store and stood to look around. Ironically the first person he encountered was George Booth's daughter Sally, who was dressed in her Co-op uniform.

"Sally Booth! What a surprise. Your dad told me you were working, but I didn't realize it was here. I haven't seen you for some time."

"I've been here a while now, Joe. Didn't see you last time you came out to the farm to move hay with me Dad. He said you were a great help. Are you shopping now?"

"I just need some information, love. Maybe you can help me?"

Sally did remember Rita as the woman who came in evenings to re-stock the shelves. "She were about my age but seemed older somehow. More worn, you know? She were odd, that's for sure. I can't believe she's dead! I felt sorry for her but she wanted no pity, wanted nothing, not even friendship. She lived in her own world and was always acting as if she was late for something." Sally pulled Joe over to the side, away from some shoppers that had just came through the door.

"I just didn't bother with her after a while. None of us did. She was just weird, like she didn't want to know any of us. And I was always waiting for her to put the tins of tomatoes in with the mouthwash but somehow she always got it right. She was always whispering things to herself."

"Did anyone ever come in to see her, or to pick her up at the end of the day? Did she have any friends at work?"

"Only a guy named Colin. He usually works the same shift, and they'd talk. They'd go outside for a smoke on their break."

"Can I talk to Colin?"

"He's not in today. I'm here filling in for him. He's been a bit funny since reading about Rita in the paper. I can check the schedule and see when he's in again?"

"That would be great, love, thanks."

Joe stood by the exit and waited for Sally to run upstairs and check the shift schedule. She wasn't long in returning with the news that Colin wouldn't be in until next week. "He had holiday time coming to him, so he took it for like, grief days, you know?"

This wasn't what Joe would have preferred to hear. Nonetheless he would have to wait the week. "I'll be back then, Sally, thanks." As he was leaving he turned back to her and added, "Please say hi to your mum and dad, and to my mom and dad as well, will you?"

Laughing, she shook her head at him and said, "Come out and say it yourself some time, you unsociable sod, you."

George Booth, Sally's dad, was an old family friend who for the last decade had lived on the farm and has worked as an assistant t his dad, Ivan, in raising North of England Mule Sheep. The sheep farm was located just past Ringinglow, a short drive away from Joe's. Ivan had always felt that George was like a brother to him, having been one of his first friends since moving to Yorkshire, when Joe was just a lad. Joe has memories of the two of them out in the pasture tending the sheep, their laughter echoing over the hills even when they were obscured from sight.

But like his dad, George had aged over the years while his duties have increased, and he now felt the need of an assistant himself. He had had a very difficult time since Ivan's stroke, as had Joe and his mom Emma. Still, George had said he has no intentions of leaving and that he could manage as long as he could rely on occasional help from Joe. And of course, hopefully one day, Ivan would hire a new assistant. George and his younger wife Olivia lived in a cottage just behind the main house. Their daughter, Sally, was now twenty and according to George, was rarely home since starting this new job.

Joe knew well the feeling of missing the company of a child after they grow up and move on. For Joe, it had at times been a struggle since losing Susan when she moved to Manchester with her mother all those years ago. Not something he would ever admit to his mom.

CHAPTER 15

Sally was not wrong. Joe had not been over for a decent visit in a long time; not since his father's stroke. Helping George with the hay a few weeks ago, he had just come and gone, waving to his dad on the porch but not stopping in to say hello to his mom. His father had been sitting on his front step, watching his son leave, a tormented look of helplessness on his face. He knew he would need to visit once Susan moved here permanently. A family dinner would be in order, which for Joe would be a chore. He struggled seeing his dad this way, since the stroke.

Joe's dad Ivan was American. He had been a traffic cop in Seattle when he met his mom Emma, having pulled her over for speeding. Emma was new to the Seattle area. She had recently arrived from England on a two-year work permit. Their courtship was brief. They married within the year and had Joe seven months later.

They stayed in Ivan's small apartment and eventually rented a small house in Kirkland. The two had nothing yet were very happy. Emma stayed in close contact with her parents, who still seemed dumbfounded by her decision to remain in America. They had never met Ivan, or Joe. Eventually Emma needed to move back home to England to tend to her aging parents. Ivan didn't mind as he had long been discontented as a traffic cop and was ready for a change, excited about leaving Seattle and having this chance to experience England.

They moved into a row house in the Hunters Bar area of Sheffield, and enrolled Joe at the local primary school. Emma's parents raised sheep and Ivan reluctantly went to work with Emma's father at the farm. It was a big change from his life in America. So began his education in sheep farming. Ivan was amazed at how much he was enjoying it. He came to love this way of life and grew quite close to Emma's dad. Sheep farming quickly became his passion.

Eventually her parents reached the age where they could no longer look after the farm and wanted to move into a nursing home. Ivan and Emma decided to take over the operation. Farms are leased from Sheffield City Council, a life-long lease. This lease can then be passed down through the generations if family members are interested in keeping it running. Ivan and Emma had gained enough experience and felt they were up to the task. They remained living in Hunters Bar until they could make plans to move. By this time, Joe was sixteen.

Their move to the farm proved a bigger task than first anticipated. The big old stone farmhouse, while glorious, was in a terrible state of disrepair. The entire north side of the large interior would need to be gutted to make livable space for Ivan, Emma and Joe. When clearing the contents of these long-abandoned rooms they had come across Emma's grandfather's diary, which no one knew existed. They carefully studied the old worn pages, which held them spellbound. He talked about the war and described the sound of the bombs falling at night in Sheffield. Gutting and rebuilding took longer than expected, but eventually they had settled comfortably into their new life as sheep farmers.

Ivan's next step was to become familiar with the sheep. These North of England Mule sheep are a cross breed of a hill ewe and a lowland ram. For example a good, hardy breed like a Scottish Blackface with good natural mothering instincts, crossed with a Bluefaced Leicester allows them to produce up to three lambs instead of just one, while being capable of producing enough milk for their offspring. As a child, Joe enjoyed time with the sheep but as he grew older, his interests began to lie elsewhere and by then he only helped out at crucial times, like lambing.

With Sally's words ringing in the back of his mind, Joe drove to the police station to check in with David. He was well aware that with each passing day the likelihood of finding the killer was decreasing. David admitted they were having the same problem as Joe - no clues. Joe had never envied David's role as a copper. He preferred the freedom of being a PI.

Theirs was a good working relationship, sharing information, but while the police often needed to deal with red tape and time constraints, Joe could roll his sleeves up and get right to work. He didn't need permission for anything, and had the freedom to bend the rules. He could even break them on occasion if he deemed it necessary. But even this had not been helping him.

He was trying to be optimistic about finding the killer. Stefan's direction seemed more towards finding the child, but Joe wasn't quite there yet. Besides, could they search for the child and be granted a DNA swab? There must be rules about that. Would it even be permitted under the confidentiality act of adoptive parents? Would it even be ethical? Joe was remaining hopeful about speaking with Colin next week. He was curious to hear what the man would have to say. He needed just one small lead. Anything.

That evening he called Janet and asked if she'd have some time to see him when she and her husband arrived in town next week. He had questions for her regarding a case he was working on.

"It's nice to hear from you, Joe. Absolutely, yes, we can speak. What's it about?"

"I can explain when I see you, Janet. Goodnight for now, and thank you."

As hard as Joe tried, he was coming up with nothing new about who would have had motive to kill Rita. She seemed harmless and there was no indication of anything devious in her movements. He was well aware of the fact that he had a long way to go. He decided it was time for him to check out the area of Kelham Island, where Rita had squatted before moving to Barnsley. Seeing the area may provide some insight. Perhaps someone would remember her.

CHAPTER 16

After a good breakfast and an extra cup of coffee, Joe drove to his office to continue the task of cleaning up his messy files. He worked with fervor, feeling a sudden urgency to get his paperwork in order. After a few days he was satisfied that the work was done. He left the office feeling pleased, and hungry again. Driving around the area in a cursory search for his assailant, he eventually stopped for a bite to eat. Looking at his watch, feeling he needed to speed the investigation up a notch, he had another thought.

Driving back to the Co-op to see Sally, he asked her if there was a way for him to contact Colin. "Here's my number. Is there any way you could get me his address or phone number?"

"You'd have to check with the day manager, Joe. And he only comes here in the morning. We don't have access to that information. He keeps it locked in the main office. Maybe you could come back one morning."

"I'll do that, thanks love."

Grabbing a sandwich from the deli, he walked out the door, running his hand through his already tousled hair, feeling a bit discouraged. His day was not productive. He had driven past the Nether Edge again but was reluctant to go in, as he really had no questions for Thomas. He would rely on his instincts in the hope that things would soon make sense.

He would need to ask Stefan about his father. Could the man be tracked down and, more importantly, could he be implicated in Rita's pregnancy?

Joe parked the car near Nonna's and got out to stretch his legs. He arched his back, walked around the block, then stopped to buy wine on Sharrow Vale Road. He wasn't clear what he was trying to achieve here, so he got back into his car and headed home. It was getting dark. It was a wasted day, by all accounts.

The shrill ring of the phone made Joe jump, jolting him to life. He had been watching the evening news on BBC, half in a trance. It was Susan calling. Mum and Alan would be here day after tomorrow, and would he like to go for a hike? Susan was thinking just a short one, from Hathersage, along the River Derwent.

"Yes, I'm always up for a hike. Also I need a chance to speak with your mum alone. It's about a case I'm working on."

"Mum mentioned it to me. That's why we thought the hike would be good. It would just mean Nigel and I would have a pint in the pub with Alan while you and Mum take your time coming inside."

Before retiring, Joe gave Stefan a quick call. He imagined that being in Stefan's shoes right now was likely a difficult thing. There was no answer, but he left a message, filling him in on what little information he had, namely the discovery of some guy named Colin, who had worked with Rita. He wished he had more to tell him, considering Colin may have nothing of consequence to say even when he did speak with him.

Stefan had remained cheerful so far, throughout this ordeal. Joe was a bit concerned as to the number of times the lad was coming to Sheffield and the hours lost while driving back and forth from Leicester. Joe was inexplicably drawn to this lad and wanted to do more for him. Stefan was only slightly younger than his own daughter and had suffered a great deal more. He knew he would not be paid, regardless of Stefan's insistence. He would never be able to afford the costs and Joe had no intention of making a profit from him.

CHAPTER 17

On Sunday morning as arranged, Joe pulled in to the parking lot beside the George Hotel in Hathersage. He had arrived ten minutes early, just in time to see Nigel's car pull up. He watched as the four of them got out of the car. He enjoyed being able to see them at a distance, giving him an opportunity to observe them, check them out. Maybe it was the PI in him. Their camaraderie and laughter made him smile. It was carefree, unburdened merriment. He could use some of that, he thought to himself. The second thing he noticed was that Janet's dark hair was cropped short. As he approached he thought it was quite becoming, although he said nothing about it.

She looked up and waved enthusiastically. Like mother, like daughter. Janet always makes Joe smile. He loved that she was a petite, tenacious spitfire, who laughed loud and worked hard. There was nothing frail about her. She had strong legs, good hiking legs, and a solid body, although not what you'd call big. There had always been an aura of confidence enveloping Janet. To Joe, there was nothing more attractive or sexy in a woman than confidence, and Janet was swimming in it. Susan shared her mother's traits. They were both vivacious and optimistic, and one could hear their laughs a mile away.

Walking up to Joe, Janet opened her pack and said, "Here you go, I brought you a present." She pulled out his favourite hazelnut chocolate bar, the jumbo size.

"Thanks, love. That's bloody brilliant!" said Joe. "That's why I love you, you always know what I need." He winked in Alan's direction.

Janet stood on her toes and kissed Joe squarely on the cheek, hugging him around the waist. "You gave us all a fright. Please be careful with this job of yours. You are important to this family."

After a quick hello all around, they set off. Joe could never understand why there was not a greater love of rambling, for he thought it was what every good Yorkshireman should be doing on a Sunday. The hike proved to be a good one, with the usual spectacular scenery that in Joe's opinion was rivaled by no other place. They set off towards Owler Tor, along the River Derwent, opting to return the same way rather than do the loop.

There was something hauntingly beautiful in the starkness of the rocky crags of the Mother Cap that sat atop the tor. Derbyshire when the heather was blooming was truly spectacular. As Joe walked, he was enjoying the stories of Janet's life in Manchester and her job at the hospital.

Alan seemed mesmerized by the scenery and was happy to walk ahead and listen to her stories. After a while he turned to let her pass.

"So Joe, Janet tells me you are quite the gardener."

"No, the gardens look crap. They haven't looked the same since Janet stopped caring for them," was his reply.

"Bollocks," hollered Janet from ahead.

"Mum's right, Alan," piped in Susan from behind. "Dad's a master with the plants, it were Mum that killed them."

"But she's a nurse, so how can that be?" teased Alan.

"You would be surprised at how little nurturing I am prepared to put into a plant," said Janet. "If it doesn't live, it's not meant to be. I save my compassion for my patients. Joe on the other hand – well, let's just say that Joe has discovered all sorts of hidden talents in the garden."

"And she rests her case," Alan laughed.

Joe stayed silent. Did Janet really just say that? That bit about hidden talents? He was thinking about the night he and Janet had spent in the garden, shortly after she became pregnant with Susan. It was a hot summer night and they'd gone to sit under the stars. Walking out onto the cool grass they suddenly became overwhelmed with – what was it? Moonlight?

It started with a bit of kissing but quickly progressed. Their mouths pressed together tightly, trying to inhale one another. Ripping at each other's clothes they ended up on the ground in a twisted ball of lust and sweat, and an animalistic craving. Their bodies were hot and wet. That night, their passion was such that it seemed impossible they would ever satisfy themselves. Their moaning turned to laughter as they realized the noise they were making.

Their laughter turned into slumber. The heat of the morning sun woke them, grass patterns on their skin where they lay. Funny Alan should bring up Joe's gardening techniques. Surely Janet didn't tell him?

Once back at the car and while the other three had headed in for a pint, Joe and Janet turned in the other direction to have a word. He knew better than to mention the garden, although he had wondered if she had thought about it as well, when she had made the comment about hidden talents. Perhaps not a conversation to have, as such were the nuances and subtleties of their new relationship. He took her arm and steered her towards the walk.

After a quick explanation of what he was looking for, she was quick to speak.

"Yes, I do remember Rita. Or Stephanie, as we had first known her. She was naïve as hell but a very determined girl. Sadly she was a vulnerable homeless child and it would have been unacceptable and unfitting for her to keep her child. When I look back, I myself had a really hard time with it all, as I know Aisha did. There was no other family; she told us she had no one. She might have lied about her age as well, and to be honest I can't even remember if she had identification, Joe. It was a long time ago."

Janet recalled another nurse whom she thought still worked at the hospital. "She was there when Rita had been told she couldn't take her baby home with her. Rita fell apart at that moment. She melted into the bed sheets and wailed. I heard the cries down the hall and came right away. I genuinely tried to help the child."

Joe was having a hard time grasping all this, as Janet tried to explain. "Homeless pregnant adolescents are a vulnerable group. Homelessness and pregnancy are huge risk factors for poor health especially in girls as young as Rita. Her pregnancy could be associated with earlier and more severe abuse during childhood, Joe. She wasn't on drugs at the time, but she could be easily led into drug use, and it was obvious she had poor mental health. She had no home, no money and no support."

They stopped walking and sat on a nearby bench where Janet continued.

"I remember her as a waif, in some ways younger than her years but in other ways not. She was an enigma. Although her mannerisms and vocabulary were that of a pubescent girl, her perceptiveness showed a street-smart wisdom. Her reading and writing skills were very poor, so employment would be difficult. She was sent back to the shelter to recuperate. Aisha was a powerful force in the girl's recovery. She was an ally, who wanted to see her come out of this situation on top. But Rita was a sad little soul who believed in dreams."

"Who knows where the child is now?" asked Joe.

"Likely the adoption agency knows. There is a process to go through, but you could find out, I'm sure."

"Thank you, Janet. That was helpful."

As they headed back towards the pub to join the family, Joe asked Janet, "By the way, what about this Aisha Hunt?"

"Aisha is a gem of a woman, always has been. I worked with her quite closely back in those days. She's been through quite a tragedy of her own, so maybe it helped her to be helping Rita."

"What tragedy happened to her?"

"It wasn't Aisha but her husband and daughter. She was married to a prominent broker, Daniel Hunt. Surely you had heard the story. It was about six years ago, I think. Daniel had dropped her off for work one morning saying he would be back at five o'clock with their daughter. He had been dropping her off for years, and a few of the girls would always peer through the windows and watch as he kissed her goodbye before she got out of the car, very loving he was. So on this particular day she talked about how they were going for a celebration after work. They were heading out somewhere special to celebrate their daughter's eighth birthday. After work, she hurried outside. She had finished up late and was concerned that she would keep them waiting. She waited a long time and eventually came back into the building, trying to reach Daniel on his phone. She was still thinking they were tied up in traffic when we heard the sirens." Janet squeezed Joe's hand.

"There had been an accident, a bad car crash. Daniel was entering a roundabout when a lorry that was veering out of control hit his car. She would never see them again. Both vehicles exploded. They were burned, Joe. The car burned up."

CHAPTER 18

Joe was driving along Abbeydale Road returning from the grocery store, always watching the people on the street, as usual. He had again been disappointed in his attempts to contact Colin. Upon Sally's suggestion Joe had gone to see the Co-Op manager. The man refused to help him, saying he wasn't too keen about giving out confidential information as Joe was not police and Colin wasn't in any sort of trouble. The boy was home ill and Joe would need to wait until he came back to work. So this would need to be put on hold for another day, although he wasn't sure Colin had any answers.

As he was turning the car towards Long Line, his cell rang. It was George Booth calling from the farm. "Lambing is almost done, Joe, but we have the last two that have just separated from the herd and my back's getting pretty sore. I could use a hand as I'm feeling a bit knackered. If I need you in the morning can I call?"

"Sure thing, George. Just let me know." He hung up with a twinge of guilt for not being more available to his parents.

Joe's dad was now seventy-three and he worried about the future of the farm. Council farms were in a large decline, and so, understandably, Ivan was unsure what would happen when he would be no longer able to run it. Since his dad's stroke, Joe had been helping at the farm more often. But his father knew most certainly Joe would not be interested to take it on. George had become indispensable.

But it was telling that George needed help, being the worse for wear for his sixty-five years. Both George and his wife, Olivia, didn't seem particularly healthy. They needed Joe until other arrangements could be made. Unloading hay was better than lambing but he realized he needed to help. A serious conversation with his dad about the farm was imminent.

Sure enough, early the following morning, George called to say one new lamb was on the way. It was a short drive to the farm and as he parked by the barn, he looked up and saw his mom come out of the house. Joe was surprised at how happy he was to see her. He was also taken aback at how old and tired she looked.

He had not given much thought as to how difficult it must be dealing with his dad lately. He walked towards her with open arms as she did the same. Dad sat on the front porch and raised a hand in a wave. Telling them both he would see them once he checked with George, Joe headed out past the barn.

Joe went straight to the field where he found George with the ewe. She was managing on her own and within minutes the lamb came. George and Joe looked at each other, a sense of relief exploding into laughter. This had been an easy delivery with the lamb helping its own birth. He was a small lamb and he wriggled himself out with only a bit of guidance from Joe, moving the hooves aside. Then they only needed to wait for the placenta. It was times like these that he reflected back to when he and Simon would do this together.

Joe and Simon would often help during lambing season, after school and again in the months following Simon's divorce. It was Joe who would help and Simon not so much. He stood by providing any necessary jocularity and assisting where he could. Simon had always seemed squeamish around the births, saying he didn't enjoy the pain and the blood. It was so much easier killing fish, as they had no visible emotion. As the years passed Joe, by now a seasoned lamber, would usually go alone.

For the past ten years or so, Simon's attention had turned to fly-fishing, mainly on the Derbyshire Wye with Vincent, his former brother-in-law. Vincent was a member of a well-known fly-fishing club and occasionally would invite Simon to fish for rainbow trout. In better days, Eva would always take the mickey out of Simon, saying he should have married Vincent instead of her. It seemed that Simon loved to fish more than anything else.

Eventually the two men headed back to the house where Joe's mom was waiting with a small lunch. Upon George's suggestion, he then called Nigel to come and check on the new lamb, as well as tend to the last ewe. She seemed ready to deliver but had been straining for a few hours now. Joe didn't realize how hungry he was, or how much he had missed his mom's cooking. It was a lighthearted visit and his dad, in a cheerful mood, was able to contribute somewhat to the conversation, adding plenty to the jocularity.

Calling Nigel had been a fortunate move, as he soon discovered the ewe was in trouble with a breach. Nigel had only recently begun his practice as a farm animal vet and was more than eager to lend his expertise. He came quickly and found George waiting for him at the house. The men walked to where Joe was waiting with the ewe.

Nigel went straight to work. It was fascinating watching the young man as he skillfully, and quickly, handled the birth. The lamb didn't have much time to be delivered once the umbilical cord was cut. The last thing Nigel checked was to make sure both ewes were nursing, and he needed to travel to two ends of the field to do this. By the time the three men returned to the house the day was gone.

Joe's mother had tea prepared for them, and it was appreciated as they were all hungry. His mom and dad had only met Nigel twice. He was a gracious, good-natured chap and Joe could see that his mom was very taken with him. She made a comment about how lucky Susan is to have such a good dad, but as usual for his mom she said naught about Janet. She was not very subtle.

"And she's lucky to have a good mum as well. Janet's been a dedicated mother, steadfast and loving," Joe retorted, with perhaps not as much subtlety as he had hoped for.

Her mother silently got up to clear the plates, pretending she didn't hear. Joe was grateful that Susan hadn't been there to hear what had just happened. Also relieved that Nigel, not knowing his mother well, would not have picked up on it.

Joe watched his mom move around the kitchen. He squinted his eyes and tried to visualize her as a young girl, cheerful and vibrant. What was her demeanour before she had been affected by cynicism and negativity? As hard as he squinted, he couldn't see it.

Driving home Joe noticed that Stefan had called and left him a message. He was going to London for a few days, to see his mom and to take Rita's ashes back to her. A difficult task, he said, but he wanted to get it over with. He said they would scatter the ashes in the yard of her aunt, as he knew she would not want to be left at the home that had driven her away.

Joe sat back and let out a big sigh. He had become embroiled in Stefan's life. He could never have imagined that finding that little body could have brought him to here, caught up in her world, knowing her secrets and feeling her pain.

It was dark by the time Joe got home. He was tired enough to sleep well, grateful that he didn't have much energy for thought. This time he left his boots outside.

CHAPTER 19

The next item on Joe's agenda was a trip to the inn in Barnsley. Although Aisha had not been certain that the place had not changed hands, he nonetheless, wanted to go. Perhaps with a look around he could find someone else who had known Rita. Driving along Long Line, he thought of stopping in at Fox House but changing his mind, he turned right at the junction.

He had received a call from Carole asking him to not be a stranger. He knew he should call her, if for no other reason than to say he was back to work and hence a little less available. He was aware of his elusiveness of late, and it was true that he had been preoccupied. But he felt like today wasn't the day to drop in on her.

Joe had first met Carole on the day when he and the lads were at Fox House watching Italy beat the crap out of England at the FIFA World Cup finals. It was almost comical to him now, as he recalled the evening. Drinks were ordered, round after round, from the new barmaid, who introduced herself as Carole. She was roughly the same age as Joe, outgoing with a nice smile. She wore black leggings and a loose flowery shirt, belted at the waist. Her heels were high, her nails were red and her wit was sharp. She liked a pint with the boys and she was not too shy to wink at Joe. She was outgoing, flirty and fun.

He and Simon had been the last two to leave, and by this time Carole had finished her shift and had joined them. Receiving an emergency call from work, Simon suddenly had to leave. Carole had urged Joe to stay, offering to drive him home. So he did stay behind to finish his pint. But Carole then ordered shots, and it was late by the time she helped Joe to her car.

For some reason, he didn't remember what had transpired in the time between leaving the pub and being at Carole's house. The last thing he did remember about that night was sitting on the floor in front of candles listening to Marvin Gaye sing "Sexual Healing." Head spinning, he sat in disbelief, taking in the surroundings. The only things missing were the beaded curtains, incense and peace emblems. When he woke up the next morning, he was in Carole's bed, her platinum hair protruding from the covers beside him. He was also acutely aware of a pair of young peering eyes not three feet away. I guess when she offered to drive him home she neglected to say exactly whose home she was going to.

After that night, Carole had claimed him as hers. She was fun to be around although Joe wasn't in a hurry to move past the casual phase of their relationship. This was not something he had gone looking for and so was unprepared for the responsibility of a girlfriend. They had fallen into this rhythm without having any real conversation about their arrangement. He sensed his hesitancy was not helping her already noticeable lack of confidence. It's not that she was needy, but felt she could be lonely in a room full of people. So while she and Joe came from separate worlds, that was the part he could relate to.

But today his thoughts were elsewhere. He planned on calling the inn in Barnsley as soon as he got home, curious to know if he would find the same proprietor that had employed Rita. He was happy to be doing this alone, without Stefan, and had been looking forward to a bit of a road trip.

It was a short call, but it did confirm that the inn had not changed hands. The proprietor and his wife were not available at present, but would be back at the end of the day, likely quite late. His sister-in-law was poorly and they had driven to visit her and bring some prepared meals. Asking if he would be available the following morning Joe was told yes, so he made his plan to proceed with the trip.

That evening, he sat watching Jeopardy in his thinking chair. For Joe it had always been a good way for him to end the day, this bit of brain teasing. At this moment Alex Trebek was staring incredulously at the answers his newest contestant was pumping out. One thing that Joe had learned about the host was that he loved it when his contestants took big risks on their betting, on the daily double and choosing the highest value clues. Big risks could easily translate into big gains. Joe thought it was a good idea to be a risk taker and realized he could maybe start taking a few himself.

CHAPTER 20

It wasn't a long drive to Barnsley and Joe easily spotted the building, a timber framed public house located across the street at the bend in the road. While somewhat in disrepair, the gardens and flower boxes were colourful and plenty, flowers spilling over the sides.

The proprietor at the Inn, Paul Darwent, was not here right now, said the bulky man who was standing in the doorway. "He will be back in half an hour, went to fetch the clean linens."

Joe walked the property gardens for a spell, pausing at the outside seating area to admire the flowers. His mother would be pleased to see how well the gardens were tended. He eventually went into the lobby of the hotel to wait for Mr. Darwent. He found an amazingly well-preserved interior, gleaming oak beams and floors. An array of bottles and jars, likely everything the man had opened in the last ten years or so, was displayed on small shelves, ledges, windowsills, mantles, and wooden ridges. They were everywhere.

All shapes and sizes, from pickle jars to clear and coloured vintage glass bottles and blue cider jugs, all neatly aligned.

Paul, a small man with a kind face, showed up about twenty minutes later. He seemed genuinely distraught at the news of Rita's death.

"She were quiet but very diligent. She were learning to improve her reading and had a lot of books. Rita kept to herself and wasn't much for talking. When she first came she hardly knew how to read or spell but she worked hard at learning. She talked to herself a lot," he said as he ushered Joe to sit at the bar. "I will never forget that, as sometimes it's like she was angry and arguing with herself." Paul shook his head sadly. "It's like there was two people inside her head and they was often disagreeing. But she were good to have around and like I said a hard worker."

"Did she have any friends? Anyone who spent time with her?"

"None that I ever seen. She would often wander into town on her off hours, I think people found her quiet. She were almost skittish, like a kicked dog, but ever so friendly. We saw Rita as a harmless lass. Worked at the food bank sometimes, would just show up on distribution days and help out. But people say she seemed to be in another world, whether or not it was remnants of her drug days."

Joe was having a hard time trying to figure out what was going on in the girl's head. The poor girl was definitely traumatized by what had happened to her and it mystified him why she repeatedly refused help. As Stefan had said, it's not like she didn't have family.

Paul continued, "When Rita found a boyfriend, she left the job. He was a no-good named Rodney, I think. In my eyes, the man were a bit of a drunk and I suspect he hit her. She lived with him for a spell in his flat but some months later she came back to the job at the inn with a few new bruises. I noticed she also had a new tattoo, must have been with that Rodney bloke, as he sported a few as well."

"Do you recall the tattoo?"

"Yes, it were a small turtle, near her elbow. The wife and I were pleased to have her back, and by then I ignored her little quirks. I think I had come to understand the girl. My wife liked her She were clean and caused no trouble. Rita stayed maybe another year after she came back, but nearly a year ago she said she wanted to find work in Sheffield. So, I helped her find work at the Nether Edge."

Just then Paul's wife came into the room. After a brief conversation, which echoed the one he just had with Paul, his wife said she was familiar with Rita's boyfriend. According to Mrs. Darwent, he lived in Grimethorpe, which was a short distance from Barnsley. The ex-boyfriend was named Rodney Hall, whom Joe was already planning to visit. It was likely Joe would go right away, as Paul's wife was kind enough to write his last known address down on a piece of paper.

Joe wished them both a good day and got in his car, heading to Burton Road. From there, he was told it was a fifteen-minute drive. He had little desire to make a separate trip to see Rodney on another day, plus he had lots of time. He was surprised at how little he knew about this area,

Grimethorpe being an old mining town that had entered a period of decline after the coalmines closed.

As Joe drove slowly down the road, he was struck with a sense of familiarity in the surroundings. He had seen this before, although he had never been here. He then noticed a huge poster in a storefront window. Pulling over to look at it, it suddenly hit him. Grimethorpe was home to the world-famous Colliery Brass Band, as was displayed on the posters that were all over the village. He had paid no attention to the posters until he had seen this large one. He remembered the movie, Brassed Off, starring Pete Postlethwaite and Ewan McGregor, depicting the band and the village. He knew the story well, as he and Susan had attended the live theatre performance at the Lyceum Theatre in Sheffield just a few years ago.

The band was formed in the early 1900's, as a hobby of sort, for the coal workers. Over the years its popularity grew and by the 1930s the band was doing radio, as well as Brass Band competitions.

"Well, you learn something every day," he muttered under his breath as he drove slowly through the streets in search of the address.

Finding parking was easy, as the place seemed a bit of a ghost town. Joe wondered if that was just today or if it was a usual thing. He walked up the sidewalk to the red brick terraced houses. Entering through the archway into the tiny courtyard, he knocked on the door. The woman who answered the door was hesitant at first to speak to Joe until he explained who he was and that he was looking for Rodney.

She seemed very young but looked old and tired. There were two young children clinging to her side and it appeared that she was expecting another child, yet she had a cigarette hanging from the side of her mouth and there was the unmistakable scent of alcohol on her breath. She said that Rodney had moved to Matlock about a year ago. Joe explained that he was hoping he could speak to Rodney concerning a former friend of his, a girl called Rita Nowak.

"Aye, we remember the breakup with Rita. The girl was smart to leave him, but I don't know anything more about the situation. Just that he didn't seem to argue with her decision. She went back to Barnsley, and he buggered off. He told us that he was moving right away, and that he would be living with his sister. Why? What's he done? Although nothing would surprise me, coming from him. I must say my husband were pleased to see his backside. He weren't the best tenant we'd ever had. Although since he's gone, we do miss the rent money. Haven't managed to find a new tenant as yet. But we aren't sorry the two of them are gone. She and him, odd ducks, the both of them."

Joe thanked the woman and was glad to be heading home. Although disappointed that he was leaving with no information, it had been a unique experience coming here. He would be sure to tell Susan about Grimethorpe and the Colliery Brass Band.

CHAPTER 21

Today was Joe's day for chores. The place was in dire need of a cleaning. Susan had been around earlier with a small bag of baked goods and he had stopped to have tea with her. It had been a productive day. The accumulating layers of dust covering everything were now gone. He had hoovered the floor and cleaned the linens. Although busy, the distractions were not enough to take his mind off the job.

While cleaning, he was listening to a BBC program regarding Sheffield's transition. Since the 1700s, the city has been building their international reputation as an industrial powerhouse in the cutlery and steel trade. Stainless steel was invented here, making cutlery affordable to everyone. Recent redevelopment has been leaning more towards arts and culture, tourism and sport. Sheffield also ranks high in education, with its two world-class universities and two colleges. "And it's bleeding crime," mumbled Joe.

What was on Joe's mind were the things that the program was carefully not talking about. Incidents in violence were on the rise in the past few years. The concern was keeping the thousands of students out of harms way. Apparently knife crimes were more frequent, with over 500 offences reported this year. In these numbers was an increase in femicide. Between 2009 and 2015, nearly 1000 women had been murdered. And as of today, the South Yorkshire Police have twenty-six unsolved murders on their books.

That evening as Joe was finishing his yard work, he heard the phone ringing in his jacket pocket, which he had slung over the shed door. He managed to grab it before it stopped ringing and was curiously happy to hear it was Stefan.

"I got back from London a few hours ago, and I'm curious to know how things are going," he asked. "I was going to text you, but I thought I'd wait until I could call."

"You first. How's your mum doing?"

It was getting dark and was threatening rain. Setting his gardening tools aside, Joe quickly headed into the house, the phone tucked under his chin. Stefan was telling him about his trip to Dagenham.

"I really hate being there, as much as I know I need to see my mum. The closer I get to the house, the more I can start to feel the tension building, first in my gut, then it works itself from there, in both directions. My head hurts and my toes won't move to walk to the front door. It seems to be okay once I'm in there. So how about you tell me your news so I can forget about my past few days?"

Joe told him about his day in Barnsley and recounted his conversations with the Darwents. He described what he had been told about Rita's life while she lived there. He then told Stefan about the subsequent drive into Grimethorpe. He shared a few tidbits of the conversation with the landlady.

While there hadn't been much to say from the perspective of the Darwents, he did mention the discovery of Rodney Hall.

"I think I need to take a drive to Matlock. I might learn something from this Rodney bloke," he informed Stefan. "He would have been the only person who knew Rita really well, and just maybe he had been in touch with her again."

"I'd really love to go with you, gramps. I'd love to talk to someone who actually knew Rita as a person and not as a homeless victim with a different name. I'll buy you lunch. It's the least I can do."

"You can come if you knock it off with the new name. You don't know me well enough to be giving me a moniker," reprimanded Joe. This was a label that he could do without, but he liked the lad.

"But I don't know you at all," Stefan laughed. "And not a chance. The name sticks until you young up."

"You know, I wish you didn't talk so much," answered Joe, feigning displeasure. Again, he found himself enjoying the banter.

"My mum used to tell me that if I ran like my mouth, I'd be in good shape," Stefan replied in playful retort.

"I have no answer for that, Stefan," said Joe with a silent chuckle.

"So, I suppose that means I'm coming to Matlock?" asked Stefan.

"Yes, I suppose it does," agreed Joe, sighing.

They discussed the arrangement. They planned to meet in Matlock on Monday, as traffic would be quieter. Hanging up the phone, Joe went outside to put away the tools. The rain had just begun.

Joe estimated it would be a forty-minute drive, an equal distance for both, so the men agreed to meet at the Fishpond in the Matlock Bath area, at eleven thirty. He welcomed the opportunity to speak to Stefan a bit more about Rita particularly following his trip back to London with his sister's remains. There may be other things he or his mother had remembered. And Joe really needed to find out more about the father. Locking the door and hanging his coat, he wandered into the front room, absentmindedly rubbing his ribs.

Joe sat in his favourite easy chair, looking out the window at the rain. It was coming down in buckets, hypnotizing him as he disappeared into himself. He put the TV on and listened to the soothing sound of another voice. While he welcomed occasional solitude, he had never completely become accustomed to the silence of living alone. Occasionally his thoughts would take him back to the morning he found Rita, lying there looking so insignificant. Except now he saw her as someone's daughter, and someone's sister. With everything that he had learned about the girl so far, the one crucial question remained unanswered. Why the hell had she been in Fulwood that night?

CHAPTER 22

Rising early, Joe called Simon. He had not seen his friend in some time and thought it would be a good day to get into the moors and have a talk. He was pleased when Simon picked up the phone. "Are you up for a hike, Sim?"

"Sorry, Joe, but I'm fishing with Vincent this morning. We are headed down to Derby Wye for rainbow trout. It was last minute. Vincent asked me just yesterday."

"Are you alright, mate? I haven't seen you in a while. Is everything okay with you and Liz? She's moved in with you, right"

"Yes, but very slowly. She's still half living with her daughter. Bloody Liz needs to do what she wants to do. Her self-indulgent daughter is not keen on this to happen. It's time Liz cut the apron strings; the girl is near thirty. I know that I have no kids, and Liz tells me that I don't get it, but bloody hell, should a kid have so much control over their mother?"

Joe had no idea how to respond to this. Perhaps the move should be delayed until Liz felt ready rather than being pushed into it. However Joe didn't know the whole story and hoped Simon could sort it out. True, Liz's daughter was just fourteen years younger than Simon and could well be living on her own, but this unexplained anxiety might be something more. He needed to find time to get together, to have a talk and see what was on Simon's mind.

Not wanting to hang up without mentioning it, Joe added, "I know I've not been around much either but let's grab a pint soon."

"Aye, we'll do it soon." A pause, and then, "Is your case a dead end then?"

"No, I'll not give up so easy. I may not solve it but I'll not give up yet. It's complicated."

Simon Hamilton lived five minutes from Joe, off Broccobank Road, behind the botanical gardens. His small locksmith business allowed him the luxury of time to himself, which Simon says was lacking in his previous career. He had retired from his security job eight years ago saying he hated being tied down to the hours preferring to come and go as he pleased. Simon was a gangly freckled strawberry blonde with wavy hair and thick eyebrows, which looked too thick and too dark in contrast to his hair. It almost looked like he adhered fake Groucho Marx eyebrows to his own.

Simon's wife had divorced him eight years ago when he was thirty-seven. This had come as a real blow to him. It left him angry and messed up for a few years. It was in these years that he and Joe became as wild and unmanageable as they had been in their youth. Carrying on like a hellion wasn't helpful to Joe's already fragile marriage. Simon never quite recovered from the divorce, although he did find a level of peace with his now girlfriend, Liz. It's only since Liz had become serious that his demeanor suggested that he was again at ease with his life.

Joe hung up the phone. Undeterred, he set off for a drive to Derbyshire, his plan being to hike up Stanage Edge to clear his head. He parked on the roadside on The Dale and made his way to the edge, eventually coming to the rim overlooking Hathersage. This truly was God's Country. As he stood at the edge of the cliff, some hundred feet above the moors below, he panned the three kilometers of gritstone rim on either side of him. He considered walking into Hathersage or to Robin Hood's Cave, but the ground was still soggy from all the rain. His boots were already drenched and encased with heavy mud.

Because of the sheer number of ramblers coming through this area, he noticed how the heather and vegetation had all been trampled into a mush of compost. He decided instead to visit his mom and dad, and to check on George and the sheep with their new lambs. He stopped at the back of his car and opened the trunk so he could change his shoes. The mud had added half a pound to each boot. Banging them together to loosen the now hardening mud, he then laced his runners, put the boots away and drove off.

But first he would stop in at Fox House. He had not seen Carole in over a week, not even so much as a phone call. He did feel bad that he hadn't called. To be avoiding her like this wasn't Joe's style. It's true that she had been subtly trying to insinuate her way into his life. He didn't dislike the idea; he just wasn't overly keen about having a girlfriend right now. She was a lovely lass, and he had no intention of hurting her. But he also had no intention of rushing things.

Walking into the pub he allowed his eyes to grow accustomed to the dark interior. He spotted Carole in the second room, standing quite close to a man, involved in what seemed to be an intimate conversation. They were both whispering and the man was stroking her arm with one finger. Carole was almost giggling. Joe quickly turned around and left the pub.

He checked his phone for messages as he made his way back to his car. There was one there from David who had called half an hour earlier saying he was at the Norfolk Arms and had Joe heard the news? David Cameron had just resigned after a failed referendum. And so Brexit was born. Joe decided to join him for a quick pint if he was still there. Maybe he had some new information about the case.

Spotting David across the room, Joe stopped at the bar to place his order.

"So you got my message. Lots going on, eh, mate? Good to see you outside of the station." David held up his pint and clicked Joe's glass.

"Sorry, I'm not feeling very witty right now," said Joe as he sat down with his ale. He caught a glimpse of himself in the mirror. It was a frightful sight.

CHAPTER 23

Monday morning arrived, and Joe managed to get out of the house in good time, successfully avoiding Rob. Joe had mixed feelings about the day, and while not particularly looking forward to the trip to Matlock he was grateful that it wasn't a weekend or at the peak of summer holidays when the bikers were at their highest numbers. What he was looking forward to was the chance to have a conversation with this Rodney bloke. His hope was to get an alibi, if the man could, or would, provide one.

There was very little traffic through Abbeydale as he passed the Beauchief, and he quickly arrived at the round-about that would put him on the A61. On the roundabout he changed his mind, taking the exit that he had just entered. He preferred instead to go back to the Beauchief and take the more scenic route along Abbeydale Road to Owler Bar and then continue along the A621. The route was slightly longer but there wasn't a lot of traffic and he preferred the scenery.

Driving the tight winding roads past expansive mountains, hillsides and windswept valleys, he was reminded just how much he had enjoyed these trips into the Derbyshire Dales. He turned up his radio and practiced on the hairpin turns that he and Simon enjoyed as young rebels. As youth, they didn't appreciate the dramatic moorland scenery, the starkness of High Tor. These days, Joe seemed to appreciate it more and more with the passing of time. Maybe he was getting old. Maybe Stefan was right; maybe he was an old codger.

Matlock Bath, also known as Little Switzerland had been a spa town since the late 1800s. While the baths are no longer in operation, the village is now extremely popular with motorcycle enthusiasts. For reasons unknown to Joe, the region's motorcycle fraternities gather by the thousands each and every Sunday during their scenic rides through the countryside. They are loud and they can be intimidating to locals and to tourists alike. While they are financially good for the local economy, they keep people like Joe away.

He arrived at the pub about fifteen minutes early and was met by a bright and chipper Stefan. Joe found the young man uplifting, his sparkling blue eyes creased with the impish grin. It was good that Stefan had found reasons in his life to be cheerful. It sounded like he'd not had a good upbringing by all accounts.

"Hi grampy." He smiled defiantly.

Joe frowned in exasperation. "I'm going to pretend you didn't say that."

Stefan didn't flinch, apparently enjoying the ribbing. "It's nice to see you too! You think I talk too much, I know.

You've told me so. Not like you, eh? You hold it all in, I've noticed. So you repress and I express. Actually, I prefer my way, so there are no surprises."

They had reached the door by then. Joe held it open and escorted Stefan inside.

"Are you always this cheerful?"

"Well, I used to be angry all the time when I was younger but I didn't want to end up like my old man. I had a teacher at school and she told me the choice was mine. She told me I needed to learn to colour my grey. So I learned and here I am, no anger left. My life is a rainbow." Stefan smiled with delight in his self-mockery, making himself tall and looking Joe in the eye.

At that point, Joe succumbed to the lad's charm. He found it impossible to not smile as well.

They settled into a booth near the centre of the interior and began to read the food board that was placed on their table.

The pub was quite small and very simple but inviting. The floors were stone-flagged and the ceilings were low. The wood beams and posts gleamed throughout. There were two men having a friendly dart game on the opposite side of the pub, and three women seated by the window, absorbed in conversation.

The menu provided an adequate selection and had both vegetarian and senior options, the latter of which Stefan suggested for Joe. Unfazed, Joe went to the bar and fetched a couple of pints of Guinness. Stopping at the kitchen window he placed two orders for the day's special, which was trout.

Their conversation didn't reveal anything remarkable. Stefan felt he had nothing more to offer. His dad was the devil.

"How did mum ever end up with a man like that?" he thought out loud before continuing, "Mum would never leave now, though, as she has amazing friends around her, for the first time ever. Her sister, Maria, lost her husband three years ago, and she gave up her home and went to live with mum. So I'm happy that Mum and Aunt Maria have each other to take care of."

Stefan stared at him and held his gaze. "What I didn't tell you earlier is that me mum is dying. She has some weird type of cancer that's been killing her for some time now. If I can make sense of anything, find some news, I think it might bring her some peace before she goes. And I don't want to lie to her. There must have been something good about Rita's life, and hopefully I can find it."

"That's not very good, is it?" Joe was shocked at this news, but felt he had to continue. "I'm sorry Stefan but I need to ask about your dad. I know you don't remember much, but have you ever asked your mum about him? Where he was from? Where he might have gone? Could he have followed Rita to Sheffield. Or worse, could he be responsible for the pregnancy? Do you think you would be able to talk to her about that?"

"I can bring it up next time I go down. I could call my aunt and ask her first. Maybe she can have a chat with mum about it."

The fish arrived and both men ate in silence, the beer having given them an appetite. The young lass that brought the plates had given a smile to Stefan, who paid no attention.

Wanting to change the subject, Stefan talked about his drive in to Matlock. He seemed mesmerized by the scenery.

"I have only travelled between London and Leicester so I'm surprised at how beautiful and peaceful it is here"

"Aye Derbyshire is a splendidly beautiful county," Joe concurred. "And if more people knew it, there would be a lot more visitors, and more cars on the narrow roads. I like it this way. The less tourists here, the better."

CHAPTER 24

Once they had finished lunch and left the pub, they made their way to Rodney's place of address. After ringing the bell the door was answered by a woman whom Joe assumed was his sister. Following a brief exchange, she pointed down the street and directed them to the hotel where Rodney worked evenings as a bouncer.

"Today is Monday, so he'll be at the pub. After weekends, he goes back in the morning to help clean up from the night before, mopping floors and taking out the trash, that sort of thing. The rest of the week he works at the car repair shop, just over the river."

Thanking the woman, they made their way to the big old hotel visible in the distance. Entering the dimly lit lobby, they were sent outside to the back where Rodney had just gone with some bags of trash.

Rodney was a big bloke, with a shaven head and liberally tattooed. Joe and Stefan craned their necks to look at the bottom of the man's chin. He clearly was much older than

Rita. Frankly, he looked too old for her. Joe made note of the turtle on his elbow, the same as the one Rita wore.

His voice was remarkably gentle when he spoke, discarding the stereotypical assumptions of a man this size. Joe introduced himself and Stefan, and then gave him the news of Rita's death. Rodney seemed genuinely surprised to hear that she had died. He was a Geordie without a doubt, speaking with a strong Newcastle accent. He was quick to say that Rita didn't deserve to die.

Inviting the men to sit at a nearby picnic table, he slowly shook his head. "She were a hard person to get close to, and she had a bad temper. But she were not a bad person. She said she had a baby, you know? A long time ago, she told me. The strange thing was that she were always on about some copper who was the dad and she couldn't figure out why he never came back. But the girl must have been mad. She didn't even know this guy's name, if there really was a guy. Who in their right mind walks around sayin' some bloke is the dad when you don't even know 'is name or whereabouts he is?"

Joe needed to pay attention to the words, to try to figure out what Rita had been trying to say.

"To tell you the truth I thought she was making the whole thing up. I don't think she had a baby at all, and I don't think she ever knew no copper. It was only when the landlady was pregnant and gave birth to her second baby that Rita started going off about having a kid. She had a scar but that could be from anything. And when I told her so, she'd want to fight, like a hellcat. She'd just start punching and hitting. So sometimes I hit her back." He paused slightly when he said it, looking over at Stefan. He gave the impression of being embarrassed to be admitting it.

Joe noticed that Stefan was having hard time understanding the accent, which was likely a good thing.

"Can I ask you about the turtle tattoos that you and Rita have?" asked Stefan.

"It were her idea. It was meant so that we would be fertile and have babies and live to be a hundred, or something like that. When you look at her now, it might as well have been a shrew. They only live a couple of years. It's kind of funny, that."

Neither man responded. To Joe, the only humour lay in how not funny it was.

"Have you been to Sheffield in the past month or so, Rodney?" asked Joe.

"I've not left here, ask me sister. Too much to do, and car's not running right now. I've been working on it at the shop but I've not had the money to buy the parts." Rodney was staring at his hands, seemingly absorbed in picking some dirt from under his fingernail. "I had no reason to go back, certainly not to see Rita. How would I even know she was living there? We didn't stay in touch; its not like we was friends or something. Besides she were too much trouble. She didn't understand things. I was glad to be done with 'er."

So Rodney did have an alibi for where he was, having not left Matlock Bath for the past couple of years and being at the job day and night. He was a dick for being so hard on Rita, but he very likely didn't kill her. He seemed relaxed and not at all like a man who was trying to hide something.

Not like Thomas King. Joe believed Rodney was telling the truth.

Rodney was still musing. "I got sick of 'er going on and on about this baby." Turning to Stefan he added, "I think that's all I'm going to say. Sorry to talk this way about 'er. She was your sister, right? I can see it in your face and your hair. She looked a lot like you. But she wasn't right, you know? She just wasn't right. I have to get back to the job now, sorry." He stood to leave; an indication that the interview was over.

Thanking Rodney for speaking to them, Joe and Stefan let the man get back to his work. Joe was deep in thought. Was there anything to this idea that Rita knew a cop?

"She should have called me," Stefan spoke at last, as they were walking back to the car park. "Why didn't she get in touch with us? We could have helped her. If there was a baby, I'd have done anything to help her find it."

Turning to face Joe, he seemed to be asking him for answers. Joe could see torment in his eyes. "Why the hell didn't she reach out to me? Did she forget she had a brother? And a mother? Did she think about what we were going through, missing her and worrying about her?"

They walked the remaining distance in silence. When they arrived at the car park a few minutes later, Stefan turned to Joe with a distressing look of defeat on his face.

"I suppose I know why she didn't call. She didn't really have a home to come back to, did she? They'd driven her out. It was because of them that she ended up where she was. Why the hell would she call them now? Why would she believe that any of them could have done anything to help her?"

Joe was grateful to be driving back to Sheffield on his own, betting Stefan was not in the mood for anything but to be alone. For the young man, this would not be a good time for conversation. He had heard some unpleasant things that must have been tough to listen to.

He turned to Stefan with a smile and gave him a pat on the shoulder, as a token of support and understanding. Stefan acknowledged this by patting Joe as well. The two men climbed into their respective cars and left the parking lot. As usual, Stefan caught Joe's eye in his rear-view mirror and gave him a goodbye wave.

CHAPTER 25

Simon's new girlfriend, Liz Crawley, was eight years older than him. She worked as a senior accountant for a large investment firm. Liz's husband had abandoned her and their daughter for another woman, taking all of the investments and his company pension. So while not destitute, she had to start with a new plan for retirement. Liz did very well on her own, thriving without the man. She had brought her daughter up alone since the girl was ten years old so they held a special bond, always taking care of each other. Liz was a brilliant lass who loved music, theatre and enjoyed painting in her spare time. Unfortunately the daughter grew up to be demanding and expecting of Liz's ongoing support.

She and Simon had met a year ago, at Nonna's of all places, over coffee. The place was very crowded one morning during Christmas holidays, and Liz had grabbed the empty seat beside Simon. They exchanged contact information and before long they were enjoying a meal in the cantina at Nonna's once a week. It was their favourite Italian restaurant in all of Sheffield. Not one of her friends could understand what she saw in him. Joe's take was that it was her business. She owed no explanation and she offered none. It was between her and Simon.

Liz also loved to cook, and on this day she had invited Joe and Carole over for a meal.

"Simon says this is overdue," Liz said with a smile, as Joe was ushered in. "And though we may not quite be ready for it, I'm always ready to have tea with our friends." Liz had not yet completely moved in with Simon but according to her, she was making good progress. Her daughter was finally warming to the idea, so no rush to get things moved as far as she was concerned.

"Still, I will never understand a child telling a parent what to do. It should be a parent has control over the child, not the other way round," expounded Simon, a little too loudly, to which the others offered no response or comment. Joe loudly cleared his throat and made eye contact with Simon. He hoped that his mate would let it go for the time being. Carole had arrived before Joe, and when he walked in to the room, she stood to kiss him on the cheek.

Aside from Simon's outburst, it felt good to be here enjoying the evening together. Joe had known Liz for many years prior to Simon meeting her, so there was a good level of comfort for everyone. He found it relaxing to be kicking back and having an evening to regroup and unwind. Liz obviously had no difficulties discussing the issues she was having with her daughter. She was a tall, full figured woman, with a big laugh and a commendable honesty.

Throughout the conversation, Carole stayed quiet, as she had two children at home and perhaps was wondering what would happen if they never left home. Would she too need to make a run for it?

Upon Liz's prodding, Joe gave them news about Rita. He didn't feel entirely comfortable discussing the case, not in such a casual environment. But he felt he could share aspects of his findings.

"I have no news, really. It's tough to know where to go from here. So do we look for the killer or do we focus on the child? Could solving one bring us to the other? But it's hard to know if the child could even be traced through child services."

Simon doubted it would be possible. "There must be rules to protect the new parents plus the child. Also you can't do it until the child is eighteen. Wouldn't this child be only about eight years old or thereabouts? Also, maybe the child was not told that they were adopted? New parents may want to keep that information confidential. Besides, why bother? It's got nothing to do with her being dead."

Joe was surprised that Simon knew so much on the subject, and agreed it didn't look good, too many obstacles. Raising his arms and folding them over the top of his head, he continued, "And yes, there really is no reason why the two would be connected. Maybe it was just a random attack. She could have been robbed; no purse was found. Or maybe it was an attempted rape. What I find the most curious is what she was doing in Fulwood, precisely near my home, beside my car?"

"That might be something that no one will ever know. The girl can't talk now, and you still have no clues," commented Simon.

The room had grown silent. Conversation had more or less come to an end, as Joe was no longer comfortable talking about the case. He sensed that Simon would not bring up anything further about Liz moving in. Joe was having thoughts that maybe it wasn't working out between Simon and Liz, although he had yet to say anything to him.

The fact that Liz's daughter had a huge influence would not sit well with Simon. Never having children of his own, he would never understand the bond with a child. He could be a real asshole sometimes and Joe could only imagine what their private conversations sounded like on this topic.

It was Liz who spoke up and quickly changed the topic, and for the rest of the visit they spoke of politics, Cameron's troubles and the possibility of a referendum.

It was late when Joe and Carole left the house. Climbing down the steps, there was an awkward silence as they made their way to their cars. He had not spoken to her since he had seen her with that man at the pub.

"Are you coming over then?" she asked.

"Not tonight, love. I think I'll head straight home. I have a lot to do in the morning. Big day ahead."

"It's about the young man Stefan, isn't it? Your heart seems in it, and he's not even family."

"Somehow he feels like family and I feel responsible, almost protective since finding the girl. If I could help him it would make me feel good. It's hard to explain, and I know it doesn't make sense."

"It only needs to make sense to you, I suppose," offered Carole.

Joe nodded. "I think about when I was his age. I had far more opportunity than him to become something, but I was useless then. I kicked around a ball and took the easiest job and hung out at the pub. Simon and I were a pair of twats. I had a home and parents who provided me with what I needed. Stefan is dealing with a childhood of abuse, a dead sister, a dying mother and he's searching for what might be his last living relative. He's on his own living responsibly and he works hard. He's far better at twenty-four than I am at forty-four."

Carole looked at him without saying a word, an expression of indifference on her face. Joe ended the conversation with, "Anyway, goodnight Carole." So with a small hug and a peck on the cheek, Joe was gone.

When Joe arrived home, he once again went to sit in his big chair in the front room, his "thinking chair", as Janet always called it. His thoughts were like electricity, keeping exhaustion at bay. Closing his eyes he went over everything he had found out up until now. He needed to find a connection. Gradually his mind calmed and the analyzing thoughts began to dissipate. Before long, he drifted off into a fitful sleep.

CHAPTER 26

Joe received a call from Thomas saying that someone needed to come to Nether Edge Hotel to collect Rita's belongings.

"I'd just finished cleaning out the room, I didn't have the strength to do it sooner. So I've got all her things in a big box. There weren't much."

"Thank you, Thomas. I'll give Stefan a call," was Joe's reply.

"But also, you said if I thought of something I should give you a call."

"I'll come and talk to you tomorrow, Thomas, and thank you again."

Joe went over the following day in the early afternoon. Thomas said he remembered Rita had spoken about a cop she knew, who was supposed to come back for her. She was sure she saw this one, about a month back. Now she hated cops because one did a bad thing to her and didn't come back.

"Where did she see him?"

"I think it were at the grocery store where she worked. She saw him there late one evening before closing time. Said she tried to run out and catch him but he were gone by then."

"How did you know she saw this man? Did she tell you? Had you ever spoken with her about it?"

"Well, no, I heard her talking on her phone one day, standing at the back of the kitchen when I came in to the room. She went quiet then."

"Thank you, Thomas, every recollection might be important. I'll call Stefan to come and collect Rita's things." With that, Joe left.

This was the second person to have said this about Rita. So, should Joe be looking for a cop? This seemed an insurmountable task, to try to link one to Rita. It would help if she had been seen somewhere with the man. Perhaps a witness had spotted them somewhere, or maybe there was CCTV footage. But where to start was the question. Now might be a good time to call DI Wilkes or David to see if there was anything new on their end, and to suggest this new theory to them.

Joe arrived at his office to meet with his team. They were working on a big case involving legal evidence gathering, Joe being one of three investigators working together. He was grateful that this was a shared case that allowed him ample free time to help Stefan. He was not obsessed but certainly determined to find out what happened to Rita. As soon as the meeting was over, he went into his office to call Stefan and asked when he could come to pick up Rita's things.

"I'm sorry to make you come out again. If it's easier for you, I can drive down with them."

"No, no, I'm good with coming," was the enthusiastic answer. He then offered a suitable time, which also worked for Joe. "I'll see you Wednesday afternoon then." Then the line went dead.

On the days that Stefan drove into Sheffield, they had decided they would meet at the offices of ARD Investigations. Joe found himself looking forward to the company of this boisterous young man with the big smile. Stefan was almost always walking sideways or backwards alongside Joe in order to be facing him while talking. And talk he did. He would describe something that happened on the drive up, or talk about his latest project at the iron shop. Joe himself would struggle to find so much to say in an entire day, yet Stefan had no problem to say as much in a single hour. The owner that Stefan was trying to buy out had been coming into the shop more frequently. Apparently retirement was not agreeing with him and the man felt perhaps he left too soon.

"This is actually not a bad thing," explained Stefan. "It definitely brings in more money when we can produce more, and also it frees me up to come here and spend time with you." He threw his arms out in a grand gesture. "So Joe, I do this for you," he said with his trademark smile.

Joe wondered if Stefan viewed him as some kind of father figure. Their relationship had been developing into something he was unaccustomed to. Driving over to collect Rita's belongings, he filled Stefan in on what Thomas had said to him, about someone Rita had described as a cop, to which Stefan replied, "So this is good, right? So rather than looking for killer, you will focus on finding the baby."

Beyond a doubt he knew what they had to do. Stefan was right. He needed to find the child that Rita had so desperately wanted to locate. It would be all that Stefan had left, once his mom passed away. "Stefan you have to realize there might not be a child any more. We need to find out what happened. But yes, we can try that," was Joe's answer. Stefan punched the air in a giant "YES."

There still remained the question of whether or not Joe could trace child adoption records through the agency. He wasn't certain he could request such in his capacity as a PI, although it might be easier since he is working on behalf of the dead girl's brother.

"If they could find the kid and perform a DNA test, would they be able to find who the dad is?" questioned Stefan.

"Yes, in theory they could, but only if the dad had ever given a DNA sample before."

After a long discussion weighing out the chances of success, they eventually decided this was the route they would take for lack of any other ideas. Plus Stefan was driving him crazy, insisting they try it. Stefan went home with a promise from Joe that he would find the files on Rita and he would call as soon as the files were made available.

Joe then called David to ask if he could order the case file from back then, was it eight or nine years ago? Joe's plan was to take this report with him to the shelter to see if any of the events could be matched up.

"Oh, and David? When you are looking, check also for a Stephanie Nowak. She may not have used her own name. And, David? Thanks."

CHAPTER 27

While trying to piece together a chronological chain of events for Rita's life, Joe tried to establish where she would have been when she became pregnant. He would call David at Yorkshire Police and hopefully start with a copy of Rita's criminal record report. Would there be any information on that report pertaining to the girl's background? Joe was hoping there might also have been an additional report filed when Rita was originally found and brought to the shelter. Perhaps some sort of sequential history of movement might be in the girl's file.

But first, Joe decided it might be helpful to go back to see Aisha at the shelter, and ask if she can remember any more details about the day Rita was brought in. Taking a chance, he calls her, saying he and his young companion would love it if she could help them again. Could she possibly find out exactly what day that was? Aisha says she cannot remember specifics, but she could get the information from June, who kept good records and also was Rita's first contact. Joe thanked her when she offered to do this for him. The conversation ended with her promising to let him know as soon as she found some news.

By the end of the week Joe was calling Stefan to come back to Sheffield. He was still sitting at his desk well past the assigned meeting time, and was beginning to think Stefan wasn't coming when he heard voices in the main office. He looked up to the door and saw Stefan walking towards him.

"Traffic is bad. There's been a bad accident, and I had to come in another way. I might have to go the long way home as well, so I'll not stay long. It's a terrible mess out there, people slowing down to look if there's any blood. Why do people do that?"

After a few minutes to let Stefan catch his breath, the two of them drove to the shelter in Joe's car. As Stefan rang the doorbell he turned to Joe.

"As I said, I can't stay long, Joe. "Sorry, we won't have a chance to talk much today. I have some things to pick up for the shop before I head back," he said.

Before Joe could reply, Aisha greeted them at the door. He turned to face her and almost lost his breath, for she seemed even lovelier than last time. She welcomed them in, offered them tea or coffee then left the room to retrieve the file. Joe looked at her with a new understanding. Maybe he noticed the sadness in her eyes. It was the look of something lost. But as she came back into the room her eyes changed when she looked over at Joe. The blankness seemed to turn into some sort of hope, possibly that she felt she was able to help Stefan. Joe wasn't certain.

Aisha had the file in her hand as she sat next to Joe. She began shuffling the papers around in her lap. "It took us a while to find the file, because like I said, we first knew her as Stephanie. But I have it now. It says here that she was found in mid-November in 2006, by a guard who was responding to an alarm malfunction." She leaned in to Joe as she opened the file to show him. She smelled like spring, like everything wonderful in the world. Her hands were fine boned but strong, with beautifully defined fingers and small wrists. She wore a pale green ring, set in a tiny band of diamonds. Joe took the paper she was handing to him.

"See here, the file notes say she had been delirious with fever, likely a flu of some sort. And she had been sopping wet and not very warmly dressed. The police were the first to receive the call, but they re-directed it to the security company, who were in charge of monitoring that alarm. The security worker who was then dispatched went to a building site out in the area of Shirecliffe. Apparently there was CCTV on the building but that was a long time ago and there would be no way to check back that far."

Reading on, Aisha turned the page. "Eventually he came upon a girl asleep in the entranceway to the offices. 999 was called, and the girl was taken to hospital. The following morning, after a brief check-up, she was held for another day. By the next morning she was considered to be in relatively fit condition. Her fever had subsided and as she had nowhere to go she was transferred to the shelter. June and I were both working there at the time. Unfortunately she was not checked for whether or not there had been sexual activity. She had bounced back quickly but had some difficulty remembering much about where she had been."

"Stefan has requested that maybe I should be focusing on finding the child. Who knows? I suppose it may give us some clues? I was hoping to have the police file as well, but I should have it by tomorrow. I can match up the two reports."

"Let me know if I can help with that. I hope you are aware this request is a little unusual, as it is usually the child who grows up and wants to find his birth mother or father. It is rare for it to happen the other way around," she replied.

"Yes, I do realize, and I will accept whatever happens," offered Stefan as if expecting her reaction.

They were scanning the rest of the papers in the file when Stefan suddenly stood up. Looking at his watch, he announced he had to leave to get back. Walking towards the door he winked at Joe and gave him a nudge as he walked past him. Joe rolled his eyes and ignored him.

He and Aisha spoke at length before Joe himself headed for the door. He thanked her, saying he owed her a dinner. She said she wouldn't have dinner with him if it were just because he felt he owed her one. He felt easy around this woman. Her disposition was engaging; she projected strength yet he found her to be calming. Walking to his car he realized that she hadn't said she would not have dinner with him.

Based on information given by Rita's mother Lena, Joe established that the events they had discussed would have taken place some months after Rita had run away from her home in Dagenham. Her mom had reported her missing after Harvest Festival. So the sexual encounter could have been anywhere between when she ran away and when she was found by the security guard. Joe found it at least promising that the likelihood of finding the child might be a lot easier than that of finding the killer.

Joe drove to the police station to pick up the file from David, hoping to find some mention of that incident. As he glanced through it, nothing jumped out at him.

"This only speaks of her arrest and there is some mention of her prostitution."

"Why don't you go down the hall to the dispatch desk. You actually need a different report. You need to be looking at our alarm and security responses," offered David.

"Thanks, I'll do that," said Joe, hardly looking up.

In dispatch records, the fellow at the desk, Jack, offered to look up the information on his computer. "Yeah here it is. It was about eight years ago now. Apparently, it was a call we received, about an alarm going off in this area. The call was re-directed to CORP Safety, who was listed as having the security contract. We usually only respond to alarms that don't have any 'who to contact' information. Later that night, a security guard had called in to report a girl to the police, having seen her lying on the covered entranceway of the new building. The site was nearing completion of construction but not yet open, so pretty deserted. Apparently, there was a big 'No Trespassing' sign posted, but a lot of good that did, eh? So, we sent an officer over who then called an ambulance. But we never got the name of the person who called it in. You'd have to call the folks at CORP."

"How about the attending officer? Do we know who that was?" asked Joe, remembering Rita's talk about a cop.

"I'll see if I can locate the report," was Jack's response. "But I'll call you, Mr. Parrott. I can't do it right now."

CHAPTER 28

"It just amazes me how much people love their pets, Dad. Don't you think?" Joe was hiking atop Ladybower with Susan and Nigel. For them, today was a welcome day off from the overwhelming duties associated with the first month of their new business venture.

"I'm not sure what you mean, Susan."

"Well, you've never had a pet, Dad, but I see it a lot. They treat them better than humans. They feed their children chips and soda pop and all sorts of junk, yet they seek out pure organic meat at ridiculous amounts of money for their cat or dog. And they verbally abuse each other and slap their spouses but would charge anyone who looked the wrong way at their new puppy. I don't get it, dad. It's opened my eyes. It seems like I've been in school for so long and I somehow missed the global shift to where animals mean more than humans. I mean, I love them, but I treat them accordingly."

"I guess I missed it as well, love," agreed Joe.

They had set off early, just as the sun was rising. Ladybower was a favourite with Joe, so Susan and Nigel were eager to join him. Taking along water and a snack on Joe's advice, they were well prepared for a very warm hike. This would be Joe's full day with the pair, starting out with this hike.

Later this afternoon he had been invited to visit the offices of their new practice, and this evening he would have dinner with them in their new flat, with Nigel cooking. Nigel had developed a love of cooking from his parents and his aunt Claire.

Joe responded, "It doesn't get any easier to figure people out as you get older, love. I've come to realize that." At that moment he was thinking of Rita and Stefan, and how it related to Susan's comments.

"I mean, you and Mum, you were always good to one another, and I felt it as well. You two had respect for each other and you taught it to me."

"Well, I will always love your mum, Susan."

"Are you sad you are not with her?"

"Actually, I love seeing her happy. And this alleviates the problem of me not making her happy. I can just sit back and enjoy seeing her be happy. Her friendship means more. I might have destroyed her if we had stayed together."

"Well she has said something the same. Do you know, she told me about the first time you kissed her, behind the botanical gardens?"

"Was that your mum? I thought it was Adele Thompson."

"DAD!" cried Susan as she playfully slapped his arm.

This was turning out to be a hot summer. From high on the ridge they could see the reservoir and how much the water had receded, the ghostly church tower now appearing from out of the water. There was once a village underneath this reservoir. Complete with a school, gritstone cottages and this church, whose spire would peek up during dry spells. Derwent Village had been sacrificed in the early 1940's for a dam, which had become necessary here in the Midlands to provide water for the growing populations of Leicester and Sheffield.

Derwent was one of two small villages that were sacrificed for this reservoir. The inhabitants were told to pack up and leave. Bodies were exhumed from the cemetery and relocated to a nearby town. Once the buildings had been demolished the water was slowly let in and people stood in awe and horror as they watched their villages disappear.

While Susan and Nigel discussed plans for a new back patio, Joe let his mind wander. Looking around him now, he could never imagine living anywhere but Sheffield. As a boy he had been bitter about coming, but now was grateful. His first act of rebellion, as a young boy back in Washington had been when he hid behind the copse of junipers in the back yard, refusing to leave the house.

His mother was angry with him, but his father had simply held out his hand and said, "Let's go son, this isn't our house any more. We've a plane to catch." And with that, they were gone.

Sheffield had so much culture, and a rich history. As a boy, one of Joe's favourite stories was that of the American pilot who crashed his B-17 Bomber in the middle of Endcliffe Park, where he and Simon used to play as kids. The plane, Mi Amigo, had been badly damaged by the Nazis while flying over Denmark, and the pilot needed to make an emergency landing. Needing to crash-land, the pilot spotted a group of schoolchildren who had gathered. He then veered the plane and managed to avoid the children, but sadly it did crash into a tree covered hill, exploding into a ball of fire, killing all ten airmen on board.

A Mi Amigo memorial plaque now stands in the park, and the men are remembered every year. The pilot was seen as a hero, as he did his utmost to avoid crashing into a group of children, instead sacrificing himself and his crew, who likely would have died anyway, as there was not room to make a proper landing. The pilot of the Mi Amigo received a posthumous Distinguished Flying Cross for his quick thinking and bravery.

Joe brought his thoughts back to the hike, as he sped up to listen to Nigel. He and Susan had been speaking of the alpacas he had been hired to tend to, and the birth of four cria that had taken place over the past few weeks. The farm has two studs and six girls, and they miraculously had four pregnancies around the same time. Nigel explained that this particular alpaca farm often sold their alpacas to the trekking places in the Yorkshire Dales.

"I think they are lovely animals, very clean and so gentle. They dislike being touched but like to be near you."

"Well, as long as you are not describing yourself, Nigel," teased Susan.

"If I were ever to become a farmer I think I could do well with them, they suit me."

"Perhaps then I might have a few baby goats. Have you seen them? The way they hop and dance?" She laughed.

"Now I know we are talking about you, Susan. That describes you perfectly."

Finishing the 5.5-mile loop, they returned to the car park in good spirits. It was warm but not uncomfortable, and the hike had been a very good one. Susan reminded Joe to be at the clinic on time and the three of them said goodbye.

With a wave, Joe pulled out of the parking lot. Although this was meant to be his day off, he still wanted to read the file he had picked up from David, and to check in with Jack in dispatch. He wanted to speak to the officer who was the first to see Rita before she was taken to the hospital. He headed to his office where he could read it without interruption. He smiled at the memory of Adele Thompson and his very first kiss.

CHAPTER 29

Later that afternoon, Joe arrived at Susan and Nigel's new practice. This was timely, as his eyes had begun to fatigue from staring at the paperwork. Driving slowly past the building, he found there was ample parking just half a block away. A low hedge of holly surrounded the small clinic and a small iron gate leading to the front door was open. Entering the waiting room, Joe first noticed the huge basket of fresh lavender on a centre table, the breeze from the open window was moving the scent around the room.

Also noticeable was just a hint of Lysol and fresh paint, but the lavender was helping. After he looked around at the white rattan chairs, portraits of pets carefully framed and hanging on the walls, and the pale blue wood trim and matching curtains, Nigel came into the room, smiling.

He had entered from the doorway behind the front reception counter, which had a wooden hand-carved sign above the frame, which read 'Parrott and Collins, Animal Medics'. An old-fashioned brass National Cash Register sat atop the quartz countertop.

"What do you think?" Nigel beamed.

"This is bloody fantastic," cheered Joe." "However did you pull this off so quickly?"

"We had a vision, and a lot of good hardworking friends. Many of Susan's old classmates chipped in as well. They have been working on ideas for months, on-line mostly. They were happy to see her moving back home so were only too happy to help."

Joe was still moving around the room, taking it all in.

"Come and let me show you the back, where Susan performs her magic," Nigel said as he steered Joe behind the counter.

The room was big and bright. There were two large procedure tables as well as a surgical table. A medical case that stood against the wall housed the stethoscopes, thermometers, anesthesia equipment and instruments. On another table beside were the weighing scales and a lot of other things that Joe didn't recognize. He was very impressed.

Soon Susan emerged from out of nowhere. "I was upstairs," she said, doing her excited little dance. "We have a small area up there that we use for storage. So what do you think, Dad?" She was beaming.

"Well done is what I think," was his response. He was duly impressed.

"Well, today we've had a good day of it. It's been a slow start but people are already spreading the word. And I did my first extractions yesterday. This lovely couple Jenny and Mitchell had brought in their cat, named Moggy. The poor thing needed her teeth cleaned, as well as a few extractions and some antibiotics. It went well and they picked Moggy up this morning. I think they were really pleased with the service. But their Moggy is old, and Jenny seemed quite upset at the prospect of losing her. I think that will be the hardest part of my job, dad." Susan was moving to the rear of the building. Shaking off the feeling, she smiled. "Come on, let's go outside."

As the three were sitting out back at a small iron bistro set, Susan and Nigel were describing how they wanted to construct a small patio area.

"This would be the perfect place to eat our lunches when the weather will permit," said Nigel.

Admittedly this would need to wait another year, once they had earned some much-needed money. Their debts had become outrageous with this project.

Joe turned to Nigel and asked, "Why Hunters Bar? Did you consider moving to a different part of the city?"

"Nigel shook his head. "No, I knew I wanted to be here. My dad has a cycling mate who lives here. He used to take us out for curry to different local restaurants, and so this area had always felt safe and familiar to me."

At last the conversation shifted. Susan looked at Joe and said, "So how are you and Carole doing? Any progress with this relationship that you two have going?"

To which Joe replied with a chuckle, "She's a lovely lass but you know, I'm okay with things as they are. I'm not in a hurry."

"Mum says it's because you've not met the right one yet."

"Mum again. How often do you two talk about me, then?"

"Oh, pretty much all the time," she teased.

"And you know, I'll not have someone else moved into our family home. I love the house. It will always belong to our memories. But I think if I were ever to get serious about a woman, I would need to live somewhere else."

"I think I understand that," agreed Susan.

"So why the sudden concern about me and Carole?"

"I dunno, really. Maybe now that I'm here and I see you, I don't like to think of you living alone over there. I suppose I didn't think of it when I wasn't here, so it didn't bother me. It's different now, me being here and seeing it."

"I think I'll know when the time is right. Things are good right now, but thanks for checking. You can tell Mum I'm good," was Joe's response.

Standing, Joe prepared to leave. He hoped to spend a bit of time at the office before driving to their home to join them for Nigel's dinner creation.

Once settled in his office for the second time this day, he sat back in his chair, twirling his pen. Deep in thought, his eyes slowly took in his surroundings. He glanced at the small collection of photos on his desk, mostly of Susan through various stages of life. On the middle shelf of his bookcase stood the small silver chalice that his parents bought him upon graduation. Unread books that he was trying to find the time to read sat collecting dust along with his soccer ball that had not been used in years.

He had all of these memories of another life and a family. He had always taken these things for granted but today he looked at them differently. Stefan had none of that. Joe wondered if he had any tokens, reminders of his life that he kept where he lived? Hearing the chatter of his colleagues in the adjoining rooms, Joe stood to join them for a while before heading over to Susan's for dinner.

Joe hadn't had many occasions to speak with Nigel and was finding the lad quite good-natured and likeable. He seemed comfortably at ease around Joe. Nigel's mixed background was Jordanian, British, Russian and Canadian. His grandfather, Omar Salman was Jordanian, having immigrated to Britain when he was twenty-one. At that time, Jordan's Christians made up only four percent of the population, and while it was not unsafe, the family felt their son would have better opportunities in Britain. So his grandfather had taken a position at the Jordanian Embassy in London, where he met his soon-to-be wife, a Brit named Gillian Quarrie.

Nigel was only sixteen when his grandfather passed away, but he remembered him as a small, modest man with a big heart. His grandmother Gillian by contrast was outgoing if not flamboyant. She was born in London and had met his grandfather at the embassy where they both worked. When they married and had their first daughter, Nigel's mother, they named her Suki Gillian Salman. She in turn had married Nigel's father Paul Perova, a Russian-Canadian. The two had met while she was studying in Toronto. They married there before returning to England and settling in Bakewell, where Nigel was born.

Tonight, Nigel had cooked a splendid meal of lamb korma that his friend Kamal had taught him. This recipe, he explained, had evolved over time with a few personal touches. Their dinner conversations had ranged from veterinarians, Nigel's parents, to his diverse cooking abilities.

The evening ended with a brief update on Stefan and their new pursuit through Sheffield City Council to locate the adoptive parents.

Joe felt tired after the wine and the korma. Standing to leave, he hugged his daughter affectionately and shook Nigel's hand warmly. He then made his way to his car. Driving at night was not something he did often these days, and he found himself mesmerized by the stars and the crescent moon in the sky. This family time had inexplicably made his thoughts turn to Aisha. She had suffered a terrible loss and was coping with the aftermath of an unthinkable casualty. He wondered how she was doing now, if she still struggled with the memories. Was she alone or had she found happiness again? Were her heart and soul still grieving? Parking his car, he made his way indoors, his face still pointing upwards towards the stars.

Joe had gone to bed almost immediately. It had been a long day and he quickly drifted off to sleep. He was awakened by the sound of a screech owl in the dead of night. The shrieking hiss startled him and he was instantly awake. It surprised him at how easily he was spooked, his nerves raw from the recent goings-on. As he lay in his bed, he felt for the first time that this house might be too big for him. He had not had this feeling since Janet took Susan and moved to Manchester.

CHAPTER 30

A nervous Stefan quietly padded into Joe's office catching him off guard. Joe hadn't heard the door open nor had he heard him enter. Stefan smiled as Joe rose to greet him. He had been waiting for this day. Joe had offered to drive Stefan to the offices of Adoption Support Services, located near the Moor.

Today, with Aisha's expert supervision, will be the day they planned to begin the process of tracing the baby's adoption. Stefan would apply on behalf of Rita, with Joe representing him. Traffic was light, and they were there in no time. Stefan stared out the window at the new surroundings in this part of the city.

Parking at the nearest car park, they walked the remaining distance to the office.

"I'm glad we get the chance to walk for a bit. I've been in the car for a spell, and it feels good to stretch my legs. I feel I'm a ball of nerves." Stefan's voice was subdued.

"You'll do fine. This part is nothing but a bit of paper. You are ready for this. Today, you will just fill out the forms and sign the appropriate waivers," was Joe's reassuring answer.

Aisha was there waiting for them and rose when she saw them walk in, immediately sensing Stefan's anxiety. The waiting room felt cavernous and impersonal but at length they were escorted into a tranquil office, with big leather chairs. Music was coming from somewhere in the walls. The shelves were lined with books and personal photographs. Behind the desk were many framed diplomas, too far away to actually read.

The administrator's name was Bob Harvey. He was a relatively small man with large glasses and an ill-fitting suit that would be more appropriate on a larger man. He was the first to speak. "Please keep in mind that this has the potential to be very distressing to the new parents. There has been an increase on social media of parents wanting to reclaim children they have given up. This is intrusive behaviour that can harm already vulnerable children. We will approach the parents, allowing them the feeling of being in full control so they do not feel pressured. You can appreciate the delicacy of the situation."

"My sister is dead, sir. I only want to know that the child is safe and well, and perhaps have the opportunity to learn a bit about him," interjected Stefan. "I don't want anything else from them."

"I'm not trying to diminish that, I just feel I need to lay out the facts," said the man. He was all business, no heart. "I also want you to know that we cannot offer you any absolutes. We cannot even suggest that you be hopeful. We can only tell you that we will try. So if we are good, I think we can now proceed."

Stefan became more relaxed as Aisha calmly and kindly guided him through the paperwork, explaining each document and going over the process one final time. Among the papers was a consent form for a criminal records search to be conducted. Stefan had also been required to give a DNA sample to confirm that he was related to the child. Once the paperwork had been completed, the administrator left the room to make copies of everything for Stefan.

Joe and Stefan left the building and walked down the street to the Rutland Arms, Aisha saying she would be along shortly to join them for a glass of lager. Joe had just relaxed his posture and loosened his tie when Aisha came in the door.

She looked pleased, and as she sat down, she smiled at Stefan. "Well then, that went well, don't you think?"

Nodding, Stefan replied, "This makes me feel good, like I'm doing something for my sister. Something that would have made her happy. It was good that life sent you my way, I think"

Joe was astounded and very impressed at how Stefan could take a bad situation and find something positive about it. He found it quite admirable. His sister was dead, yet he found reasons to be happy, as in trying to find the child.

The conversation turned to Aisha and how she had come to love this line of work. As Stefan had earlier described, it made her feel good about doing something for people who lacked the resources to help themselves. The visit was a short one, Aisha finishing her beer and excusing herself. Joe invited her to join them for dinner but she politely declined, saying she had a late meeting she needed to attend.

"My mum would be happy to know there's a baby, a part of Rita living on," said Stefan between mouthfuls. He and Joe were currently seated in a noisy little Indian restaurant on Banner Cross Road, Joe eating his lamb bhuna, Stefan devouring the chicken biryani. Nigel's curry had left him wanting more. He had a penchant for Indian cuisine and was happy to find that Stefan enjoyed it as well. "But I don't want to tell her if I don't know for sure. It would be nice if I could bring her the news one day, before she goes."

Joe had questions for him that needed to be asked. He had been putting it off but now seemed as good a time as any. But first he waited until Stefan finished.

"Lately I've been thinking about what my life might look like in five years and I've been thinking of making some changes. I will go see Mum while she is alive, but then I need to make decisions about how I want to spend the rest of my life. And about whom I want to be. I know that I like coming to help you with your inquiries. My old partner has been hanging about, saying his life was lacking something, and he perhaps retired too soon. I don't want to be in that rut one day."

"Stefan I need to ask you to do something for me. Did you get a chance to ask your mum if she knows where your father went? And do you know if there are any of your dad's belongings still at your mum's? I'm talking like a hairbrush or a toothbrush, or a piece of clothing that might not have been washed? She might have thrown everything away, or she may have put his things in a box, thinking he might come back. I don't know."

"You want his DNA?"

"Listen, we need to rule out that he could be the father. And we need to rule out that he didn't come here to find her."

"You think he might have killed her?"

"No, I don't. But we need to rule it out."

"Okay Joe, I've not done it yet, but I can ask her. And don't worry, it doesn't bother me none. I didn't ask earlier because of upsetting her, but I will, I promise."

Dropping Stefan back at his car, Joe shook the lad's hand warmly. "It was a good day, Stefan, and hopefully you will have some good news soon." Stefan looked tired. He was putting a lot of himself into this venture and Joe hoped he would go home and get some rest.

Driving home Joe turned up the music, which was unlike him. He usually listened to BBC Radio talk shows. But tonight he sensed some kind of calmness in the air. There was a beautiful sunset on the way home. The kind where dark ominous clouds edged with brilliant white are set against the gold and red hues of the sky. Imposing shafts of sunrays were glowing down to the earth, conjuring up images of outer space or God.

When Joe got home, he picked up the phone and dialed her number. When she answered he spoke, "I know I didn't ask you properly last time. In fact, I didn't really ask you at all. I didn't mean to say I'd buy you dinner because I owed you. I'm a bit out of practice at this, so you'll have to excuse me. What I meant is that I'd love to take you to dinner. So, I'll try again. Would you like to have dinner with me?"

"Yes, I will have dinner with you, Mr. Parrott. Joe," was Aisha's answer.

Joe smiled as he hung up the phone. "Don't call me an old codger," he mumbled to the absent Stefan.

CHAPTER 31

Joe is parked outside the Nether Edge. He has been here for almost an hour, watching people come and go. It was early morning and there were lots of people about. He had yet to discover any motive for Rita's death and was finally accepting the fact that it may have been a random act of violence, and the location could be nothing more than a coincidence. Perhaps she was just out for a bike ride? He had no idea in which direction she had been traveling at the time. Perhaps she was looking for a new job at one of the local businesses? He would check at the Fulwood Co-Op and the two neighbourhood inns to see if anyone there recognized her, or perhaps had heard from her. But still, why did Joe have the feeling that Thomas was acting suspicious?

His phone rang. It was Stefan calling to tell him he was on his way to London and he'd be gone for a few days. His aunt had called to say that his mom had taken a turn for the worse. This, he had said, was also a good opportunity to take Rita's box of belongings back. They would go through them together.

"It will be the perfect opportunity to ask her about my dad, although I don't know if she will want to talk about him. And of course, I can't tell her why I want to know."

Joe was stirred by Stefan's care and commitment to his ailing mother, despite how he judged her about his upbringing. He had said it was hard to pin blame on her as he put it down to the fact that it was beyond her capabilities to be a parent.

"I know absolutely nothing of her background, how she was raised or where her parents had been when me and Rita were young. When we asked about grandparents we were told that they were gone. It was the same mystery with my dad. I wonder what she can tell me about him."

Joe hung up and rolled up his window. The breeze had picked up. He started to wonder why he was still sitting there but decided to wait a bit longer. Seeing nothing of interest as the clock ticked away another thirty minutes, Joe slipped his keys into the ignition and started the engine. His phone vibrated in the cup holder and he saw on the display that it was someone from the Yorkshire Police Department calling.

"Hullo, Joe? My name is John. Constable John Francis. I heard you were looking for me, about an alarm callout from eight years ago. I'm the one who was dispatched when the girl was found. Do you want to have a word?"

"Yes, thank you, John. Where are you now? Can we meet?"

"I've just come on shift, here at the station. Maybe you wouldn't mind stopping by."

"I'll be right there. I'm not far away." Joe was already driving before he hit the disconnect button.

As Joe walked up the steps, he noted how stiff he was. He had sat too long in the car. He needed a good long walk. The constable was waiting by the front counter when Joe walked in. Ushering him to one of the interrogation rooms, the two men sat down on the same side of the table, turning their chairs slightly to face one another.

"This won't take long," Joe assured him.

Constable Francis was a youngish looking man, perhaps in his early thirties. His demeanour was very somber and business-like, seeming to take this issue very seriously.

"I remember seeing the girl lying there, so small and wet, this big old coat was only half covering her. She seemed high on something, but when I touched her forehead it seemed more like she was burning up from fever and could have been delirious. I reached down to try to wrap her coat around her but she started to cry and say, "No, no, I can't do it," or something like that. She was pushing my hand away and covering her face. I hadn't been a copper for very long and I had never had anything like this happen to me, so I called dispatch to send an ambulance."

"And I imagine you stayed with her?"

"Yes I did. The security bloke was already in his van ready to drive away when I got there, so there was nobody else to see to her. He pointed me in the right direction, then he drove off."

"So, police got the call, passed it off to security, who again passed it off to police? Brilliant." Joe's comment was more sarcastic than he meant it to sound, but it was inconceivable how everyone involved had so little concern for the girl who had been lying there on the ground.

"She was likely a squatter, not uncommon, so we didn't pay much attention, other than to get her away from the building and conclude the callout," the man answered, almost apologetically. "There was not really anything else we could have done."

Thanking the man, Joe left the building, wondering if anyone else had seen Rita before she ended up on that doorstep. He needed to make a trip to CORP and find out who it was who took the call and attended the scene. He made a note to call in at the organization as soon as he could find the time, sooner rather than later.

As Joe was turning the car around, his cell phone rang again. He had never known it to ring as much as it had lately. The display read ARD. Someone from his office was trying to reach him.

"Ey up, Joe. It's Barry. We were waiting for you to come in, but weren't sure you were planning on it today. Two of our lad's wives had rented a booth at the Nichols and today is their grand opening. We are all popping in to show our support and then we were all off to the Prince of Wales to watch the football match. Are you coming, Joe?"

"I can come, Barry," was Joe's enthusiastic answer.

"So you can park at the Prince of Wales and I'll pick you up. We'll drive out to the Nichols then back for the game. Can you be there in an hour?"

"I'll be there, mate. Appreciate the call." Perfect timing, he thought, as he again turned his car around to head in the opposite direction.

The Nichols building, a grand old Victorian red brick structure was built in 1854 and was once a grocer's dry goods warehouse but now serves as a huge vintage empo-rium selling furniture, glassware, ceramics, old records and the like. Studio flats were now rented on the top floor. To have obtained space in this building was indeed an accom-plishment. Joe marveled at the pieces of furniture set out by these two women, the wives of his mates. He had never met them before, but was impressed with what they had accomplished with their grit and determination. These were pieces that they had collected over the years while driving the counties of Yorkshire, Lancashire and Lincoln. 'From second hand shops and roadside giveaways,' they had explained. This included tables, chairs, benches, and small nightstands that they then took home and restored.

The reconditioned product made evident the amount of labour that would have been involved to restore these pieces. While most were not antiques they were beautifully fin-ished, some natural while others had been intricately hand painted. The items would be an eye-catching addition to many a room. They lingered longer than they had planned, and before long were on their way back to Ecclesall.

Joe, Barry and the rest of the boys made it back to the Prince of Wales just in time for the football match to start. Joe grabbed a pint at the bar and joined his mates who were seated around a cluster of three tables. Just as the match started, Joe looked up at the sound of a familiar voice. It was Simon, coming towards him, a look of surprise on his face. He had walked from home, saying it was time he started getting back into shape.

"Are you here to watch the match, Simon?"

"Aye, I am, man. Just like old times, eh Joe?" Simon laughed.

"Yes, it feels like that," agreed Joe. This had become a great evening, sitting here watching a smashingly good game with his best mate. It wasn't a late night and Joe drove Simon home when the game was over.

CHAPTER 32

Joe was scrutinizing the contents of his refrigerator when the phone rang. He had been trying to decide on the half can of beans, the piece of cake or the tuna casserole. He shut the door and picked up the phone. Bob Harvey from the adoption agency had made progress and had new information, but Joe would need to come and see him in person. Joe made an appointment for the following day. Hanging up, he then continued his quest for something in his fridge that was possibly still edible.

Arriving promptly at the assigned time, Joe was soon seated in Mr. Harvey's office. The man cleared his throat before he began to speak.

"Well, the news is good. Our agency has indeed located the couple that adopted your client's baby. They were very receptive to the contact, and didn't hesitate to speak. As a matter of fact, they were extremely receptive to the idea, which I must admit did surprise me. This is their only child and yes, they had planned on telling the child that he was adopted. They said their plan was to tell him when he turned sixteen."

"So this is very good news then?" asked Joe.

"It certainly seems favourable. They have agreed to talk to you Joe, but Stefan cannot take part in this call; only you as his representative. I hope you understand, as at this point, it's still anonymous and they need to protect the rights and privacy of themselves and the child. So if you would sign this form we can go ahead and arrange a conference call, to be held here, between you, the social worker, and the parents. That is, if they don't change their minds. That happens sometimes as well."

Agreeing, Joe made the necessary arrangements with Mr. Harvey.

The time flew by. He was back a few days later as arranged, and within a few minutes he was seated in a conference room with Mr. Harvey. "You are on speaker phone, Joe, so as soon as you hear them pick up at their end, you can begin speaking," instructed Mr. Harvey.

The phone was answered on the third ring and Joe began speaking. "Good morning, Mr. and Mrs. Dwight. My name is Joe Parrott." He spoke clearly and succinctly. "I think you know why I am calling."

"Yes, how do you do?" came a nervous sounding male voice on the line. "I suppose you'd like to get right down to it, so we can be clear of what it is you want?"

Joe cleared his throat. "Yes. Thank you. I am a private investigator representing a young man whose sister was brutally murdered, as you've been informed. We believe your son is very likely the child of this woman. I graciously ask you if I can come and visit you in person. I'd like very much if you would permit a DNA sample to be taken on behalf of my client. This of course would be handled in the strictest of confidence. You see, he needs any kind of closure, confirmation of the relationship to this child, possibly a way to trace the father. And during the course of this, we can perhaps even find the killer."

The woman spoke first, introducing herself as Elaine. She expressed the utmost respect for Stefan's courage and integrity in pursuing this on behalf of his sister. It was commendable for a young man of his age. A long conversation ensued with Joe telling them what he knew about Stefan since meeting him only a short while ago. Joe was pleasantly surprised at the way this was going so far.

"Joe, Mr. Dwight here. I think it would be most proper if you could come here, to see us in person. We would prefer the anonymity at giving a sample directly to you, on behalf of your client so that we don't need to deal with another agency out here. The less people involved, the safer I would feel."

"It would help if you yourselves, within the next few days, could take some sample items for me. Perhaps nail trimmings, or ear wax on a couple of cotton swabs. If he has a runny nose, perhaps you could place a used tissue into a plastic bag, or his toothbrush. Please leave it to dry and then place it into a baggie as well. We could use hair, but it would need to be pulled out at the root, and I don't know if that would be a possible thing to do."

"Yes, yes, my wife has written that down. We will see to it."

Joe was pleased by their positive and easy responses. He offered to drive to Cottingham at any time that would be convenient to them. Without thinking, he brazenly offered to come the next day. They readily agreed, which surprised and pleased him.

"We were horrified to hear of the death of the birth mother. We are more than curious to speak with you. And if it would help with the murder investigation we would be happy to do this."

"I am overwhelmed with appreciation, Mr. and Mrs. Dwight, truly."

"Elaine is oddly excited about doing this. She has good judgment and I'm with her all the way. We look forward to speaking with you tomorrow, Mr. Parrott. We would like very much to see some justice done, on behalf of our son."

As he hung up the phone, he could see Mr. Harvey, smiling. "Well done, Mr Parrott. That went extremely well. It seems the child has found himself some very decent parents."

It was the first time he had seen the man smile. Mr. Harvey then leaned over and handed Joe the Dwights' information card. The notes on the card reveal that the couple, Liam and Elaine Dwight, lived in the area of Harland Rise in the village of Cottingham, just outside of Hull. Liam worked in engineering and Elaine was a barrister of Civil and Regulatory law. Joe could still hear her words on the phone when she said it would be invaluable for them to know something of the birth mother and her brother. Joe wanted to high five himself. Stefan wasn't here, and Mr. Harvey didn't seem the high-fiving type.

He planned to leave early in the morning. Driving home, he called Stefan to give him the news. The young man could scarcely contain himself. He wanted to go with him but Joe said no.

"You need to understand that at this point, I am bound to the non-disclosure rules. All decisions will need to be made by the parents. They will decide if and when you will meet them, but of course, the DNA will need to be done first, to authenticate your link to the child."

"I don't know what to say to you, Joe. Thank-you doesn't seem enough."

"Yes, thank-you is enough, Stefan. I feel very good about doing this, believe me." And with what felt like a lump in his throat, Joe hung up.

Poor Rita, all this time wanting to find her baby, wanting to know of his whereabouts and that he was being taken care of. And now that it was happening she was no longer here. Stefan, wanting to find the baby on behalf of his sister, would need to wait a little longer for the outcome of the meeting. It was with acute awareness that Joe was watching this unfold.

CHAPTER 33

Joe headed off to Cottingham full of optimism. Google maps brought him directly to the front door of a delightful detached brick house on a corner plot. He parked in front of the house, took a deep breath and exited the car. Walking up the sidewalk, he raised his hand to knock on the door when it suddenly opened. Standing there were two smiling people, likely in their late thirties. Both were clad in denims and t-shirts. Elaine had honey-red hair cut in an attractive bob worn just below the chin. Her fringe was long, almost covering her eyelashes. Liam was tall and slim, with dark brown hair worn long and loose, tucked behind his ears. Without delay they invited him in to their house, which looked as charming inside as it did out.

The place was immaculately clean and very modern. The walls were a soft, almost mint green and contrasted by a rose-coloured sofa set and white window trim. Joe was led through to the back of the house, into a brightly lit kitchen. The wooden floors gleamed. They invited Joe to sit at the table. The pine dining set was situated in front of a large window adorned with colourful curtains. Visible through the oversized rear window was an attractively decorated yard, completely fenced with playground equipment.

As Joe lowered himself into a chair, he heard a voice behind him.

"Hullo."

Turning, he found himself staring at a child who had come into the room, and had walked directly up to where Joe stood. Joe instantly noticed the resemblance to the Nowaks.

"Hello, young man. And what's your name?" asked Joe

"Aidan," the boy answered, as he held out his hand to shake Joe's. "How do you do?"

"Aidan," repeated Joe. "That's a brilliant name, isn't it then? And I'm Mr. Parrott."

"You mean like a bird?"

"It's a people name that sounds like a bird, that's all," Joe tried to explain.

"I'm the only Aidan on our football team at school," he said proudly, already forgetting about Joe's name. "And I'm one of the tallest boys. Mum says I've just had a growth spurt." Aidan abruptly made himself tall.

"Soon, you will be as tall as me," offered Joe.

"I might be taller than you, Mr. Parrott. Do you want to see my Lego robots? I have two that are motorized."

"Sure, I would. Would you like some gum?" offered Joe.

Aidan looked over at his dad, who nodded his permission to take the piece offered.

" Yes, please. My dad says gum is okay sometimes."

Aidan brought his robots and carefully explained what they were. Elaine brought cups and Liam followed with the tea. They sat down at the table opposite. Once Aidan had tired of the new visitor, he took his toys and retreated to his room.

Joe looked up at Elaine. She had soft blue eyes. Her skin was pale but for her rosy cheeks and pink lips. She had a healthy glow, almost an aura around her.

"You could almost pass for Aidan's mum," Joe found himself saying. He then instantly regretted it. "I hope its okay that I said that."

Liam looked over at his wife and smiled. He seemed to care a great deal about Elaine and Aidan. "She has been told that before, Joe," he responded with a big smile and kindness in his eyes.

Not wanting to overstay, Joe finished his tea and stood up. Elaine handed him a small bag. "Inside you will find Aidan's toothbrush, a small baggie with fingernail clippings, and that chewed up piece of gum that he just spit out."

Joe had his necessary samples for the DNA test. He thanked them both and walked back out the way he had come in. The Dwights accompanied Joe outside to his car. He took one more look at the house, and at the little boy peering out at him through the curtains. He gave a smile and a wave as the little face disappeared from sight.

Though slightly worried at pushing his luck, Joe turned to them and asked if they would be willing to speak to Aidan's uncle. "Not right now. I realize it's too soon. But perhaps once all the tests are done and we can confirm the relationship. We can arrange something on Skype, likely from my office. This may not be of consequence to you, but his mum is dying. I think he'd like to let her know that

Rita's child is well. Aidan will become his only relative, aside from a very old auntie. I can certainly vouch for the man's character."

"We will give it some thought, Joe. We have some time to discuss it. But yes, we would like to meet him at some point. Just perhaps not right away. Elaine also has no living family, having just lost her brother to cancer."

Elaine agreed. "Yes, we'd love to meet him eventually. I myself was adopted so I'm aware of the importance. I never knew my birth parents. My adoptive parents were Irish, like my husband. We named Aidan after my father. They are both gone as is their son – my brother." Realizing she was talking too much as Joe was trying to leave, she smiled and added, "I'm sure we will speak again in the near future. Have a safe trip home."

Driving back to Sheffield Joe thought about the similarities between the Dwights and their new son. Elaine herself had been adopted, and neither she nor Aidan had known their real mothers. Also both had prematurely lost all their family. He was overcome with a huge feeling of accomplishment. This made him feel really good inside, regardless of whether or not they'd find the killer. Stefan was right about that.

CHAPTER 34

Joe got up early. Throwing on a pair of jeans and a t-shirt he got into his car and drove to Nonna's. He wanted to have a coffee with Simon, and Nonna's was the most likely place to find him. Sure enough, he was in his usual spot, newspaper in hand. Simon looked up and nodded at Joe as he walked over to the barista to order his cappuccino. Joe then brought the coffee over and sat in the stool beside him.

Just as Simon was saying hello, Joe's phone rang. It was his mom, Emma.

"Dad is sick, Joe. He was just taken to hospital, I think he's had another stroke."

"Gotta run, Simon, it's me dad," he shouted over his shoulder as he ran out the door. "Here, have another java."

Joe's mom was waiting for him at the main entrance to the hospital. She seemed calmer now, after having received an update from the doctor. It seems Ivan did not have a stroke. It was more likely heart palpitations due to anxiety. He hugged his mother and together they headed for the elevator.

Joe walked into his father's room. He was asleep. Joe touched his dad's shoulder and whispered hello into his ear. He then went back to the waiting room where his mom was sitting waiting for him.

"Is he still sleeping?" she asked.

"Yes, I'll come back later."

"I hear you saw Janet when she were here."

"Yes, Mum, we always try to get together when she and Alan are in town."

"I don't know why you bother with her after what she'd done to you."

"She didn't do anything to me, Mum. It's what we each did to ourselves."

"She took Susan away from you."

"No, Mum, she didn't. I have always had the freedom to see a lot of Susan. Besides, a girl needs her mum." Joe had no intention of getting into this right now. He stood to leave. "Bye, Mum, love you. Let's focus on Dad right now, okay? I'll check back later today."

Joe was trying to remember what a normal day had looked like. He had lost all sense of routine. Perhaps he never had a routine and had just realized that he was in need of one. The elevator bell rang to indicate it had reached the lobby. He left the building feeling tired.

Just then, Joe heard his name being called, and looking up, he saw George and Olivia Booth in the parking lot, walking towards him.

"Dad's sleeping right now," he said to the pair. "But he might wake up by the time you get up there. I'm off, but I'll be back later."

Hang on a bit, Joe. Sally's just parking the car. I think she wants a word with you."

Joe stood on the curb as Sally walked across the roadway towards him.

"Your dad said you want a word, Sal," said Joe as he smiled at her. It was a smile he wore gingerly in a brilliant display of mock buoyancy.

"I do want to talk to you, actually. It's about your dead woman case. I was speaking to one of my work mates and she remembered something that happened about a month ago. She was working with Rita, on their knees unpacking small boxes, and suddenly Rita jumped up. 'That's him!' she had yelled, and ran out the door. She was gone about fifteen minutes and came back in crying, saying, 'I know it were him, I know it were.' So what I'm saying is that maybe your guy is not that far away, Joe."

"Thanks Sally, I'll want to speak to that girl." As he walked away he didn't bother trying to smile. Joe realized he wasn't just tired. He was done in. He needed a diversion. He drove to his office. He had a message from a potential client regarding an insurance fraud. He would need to call him tomorrow. He left the message on top of his desk in plain view, where he'd be sure to see it first thing.

Later that day as Joe sat by his father's bed, his eyes were on the television located high on the wall. He had been there for hours, although the two hadn't spoken more than twenty words, so drawn were they to the screen. The BBC breaking news was reporting a terrorist attack at Port El Kantaoui in Tunisia. It was beyond tragic. Thirty-eight people were killed, thirty of whom were British. Joe always wondered why they said that. The nationality should make no difference. People lost their lives.

The gunman had then fled into the street where police shot him. "Good for the police," he said to his dad. A much bigger deal than poor little Rita but all deaths were tragic.

"Look at me, lying here in this bed. We live our entire lives trying not to die. But we all do. We don't need anyone coming along helping us to do it any quicker. We should never die before our time."

Joe agreed.

"I remember your grandfather, Joe, when he was dying. He was ninety-two years old and he just looked at me and said, "Somehow it's never enough." That was the way he was. And what he said is the truth."

Joe rarely heard his dad speak in such a reflective manner. "Dad! Did you hear yourself? You are speaking better now than you were last week. Maybe this attack brought your voice back. Or do you think it's the drugs?" They were laughing when Joe's mom walked in. This was his exit cue. Kissing them both, he left the room.

Before the world went totally mad, Joe would love to go away. Maybe back to Honfleur, France, where he and Janet went for their honeymoon. Or maybe he would go to America to visit his aunt and uncle, and his cousins. Since moving here as a boy, Joe had never been back. Perhaps his cousins could show him some policing techniques used in America. The more he thought about it the more he found this a good idea. He got into his car and headed for home. He had a dinner date to get ready for.

CHAPTER 35

Joe waited outside the restaurant for her to arrive. Aisha had insisted on meeting him there. He stood there, nervously watching both directions. Then he saw her coming down the walkway. She had an easy gait and seemed to be gliding. She wore long, loose trousers and a fitted wrap-around blouse. Her jewelry was simple and her heels were just high enough. Her hair was wrapped in a loose bun at the back of her head and she was wearing a hint of lipstick and a big smile.

"You're looking very Amal Clooney," he said to her.

Aisha rolled her eyes and shook her head, feigning displeasure at the compliment. "Well, I'd love to be able to say you look like George Clooney, but…"

"But?" asked Joe.

"I was actually going to say you look like the little plastic man in the dumpling commercial. On the telly." He could see the amusement in her eyes.

"Okay, you got me. Say no more," he said as he took her by the elbow and guided her to the door.

They were seated at a small candle-lit table for two by a window. The panes were cut glass letting in the light but screening visibility. The room was comfortable, the music was at a good volume and the atmosphere was vibrant.

They spoke briefly about the case although neither of them wanted to discuss work while out socially. Joe was eager to tell her about his visit to the Dwights' home. They ordered wine and when the waiter brought the bottle, he left the menus. By this time, their conversation had broken away from the case. Joe found himself telling her things about himself. He was amazed how easily he spoke around her, with candor. He even felt comfortable confessing that no one had hired him since his accident. With Aisha, he no longer cared if he seemed less than perfect, to show his flaws. Learning more about Rita and Stefan was teaching him that.

On Joe's urging, she talked a bit about herself. Her parents still lived in her native Luxembourg. Her father was a classical pianist and she begged him until he taught her to play. She attended the "Kinnekswiss loves…' event last July, and found it to be spectacular. She tried to go every year.

"I don't know what that is," commented Joe.

"It's an open-air concert with the Luxembourg Philharmonic Orchestra. My father used to play there, with the orchestra and sometimes as a guest. The event is an overdose of classical music with guest musicians and singers. The performances are always exciting. But I also have a brother who sings in a punk rock band. I've been to a few of his concerts, one in Amsterdam and the other in Dublin. I try to go whenever I can, depending on where they are." She took a sip of her wine before continuing, "But me, I tend to lean towards jazz and, of course, Mark Knopfler."

"Would you ever move back there?" asked Joe.

"No, I love living here. I have a home in Derbyshire, in Baslow, where I lived before I met my husband. I've kept the house; its been rented out all these years. But I hope to go live there again one day, when the time is right. I'm almost ready to sell the family home here in Sheffield and live there full time. The area reminds me of home without having to go home. I love the moors, the textures and shades of the land. I never get tired of seeing the colours–the richest of green and the blackness of the tors."

Joe smiled at her. He felt the same about the area. "Do you see your family often?"

Aisha nodded. "Yes, my parents and brother come once or twice a year."

"I've wanted to ask you; you have a beautiful name, where did it come from?"

"It's Arabic, I believe. It means 'life.' Apparently, it was the name of the Prophet Mohammed's third and favourite wife. Don't ask me why my parents named me Aisha; my mom just said that they both loved the name. There's a beautiful song out called "Aisha," did you know? By a famous singer Cheb Khaled, and a version by the Gypsy Queens. It's a great song, really!"

Joe smiled. "I'll be sure to look it up."

After a brief lull in the conversation, Joe spoke. "So we've covered a good part of your life. I'm sorry I hope I wasn't prying."

She looked up at Joe and held his gaze. "The rest of my life I'm not ready to talk about, I'm afraid. Nothing lasts forever, does it Joe?" she said at last.

The waiter arrived with their meals. He was a jolly man, Jamaican with a strong accent. His humour broke the seriousness of Aisha's last comment and put them in a lighter mood. Aisha generously peppered her food.

"Tell me a bit about yourself, Joe. Were you born here in Sheffield?

"I was born in America. Seattle, Washington. Land of lumberjacks and airplane parts."

"And the Dave Matthews Band," added Aisha with a big smile. "Crash," she whispered.

Joe laughed. "Yes, but nothing as glamorous as Luxembourg. A lot of big trees and a lot of rain." Joe was trying hard to sound cheerful.

"There's nothing American about you."

"I came as a boy so my more formative years were spent here. I remember very little about life there."

"I was surprised when I heard that you and Janet split up. I thought you were both very happy."

"She told me I was acting too much like a detective and she wanted to split up. I said good, we could cover more ground that way," said Joe, trying for continued levity.

"You don't tell very good jokes, do you?" She looked at him, half serious. "Maybe you should leave that job to Stefan."

"Well, that's probably why she left me, then. It was the bad jokes." On a more serious note Joe added, "She saw the writing on the wall before I did. A woman's instinct is often stronger than a man's reason."

"So that leads me to my next question. Do you like being a PI?"

"I think so although there are days I wish I did something else. As you may have noticed, I'm not always good with people. I don't do it consciously; it's just the way I am. So its often better I work alone. I just hate to think that I'm not as smart as the crooks."

They both laughed and turned to their meals.

The evening passed by far too quickly for Joe, but he knew it had come to a close. By the time they left the restaurant, they were walking closer to each other than they had been going in. When they reached the corner, Joe gently kissed her on the cheek, and then Aisha walked away.

CHAPTER 36

Joe spent a good part of the morning visiting some of the businesses in the Fulwood area. He had a picture of Rita and he had been asking if anyone knew, or recognized her. Maybe she had been in seeking employment. Every turn drew a blank. Nobody had recognized the girl. This again left Joe feeling somewhat defeated.

The previous day he had been to Kelham Island but soon realized there was nobody there who could help him. Based on Aisha's description of the area six years ago, it looked very different now. He imagined it had changed considerably since Rita would have been here. The pervy blokes who would hang around, drooling over the young girls, were mostly gone, as were the girls. With many new businesses and upscale pubs, the area had improved a great deal. An increase in the amount of people moving about added to the improved face of the area. Many of the hookers had moved on to the areas of Neepsend and Shirecliffe, where one could still spot used syringes and girls looking for johns.

It was not that long ago that dozens of men would have been arrested on these streets, and over a short period of time. The number of men trying to buy girls for sex was once staggering. One had been a professional footballer and another a special constable. It was far more likely the curb crawlers would get arrested rather than the prostitutes. The girls would be right back if taken away, so there was no point. There was a greater chance for them to be arrested for drug offences and not prostitution.

Joe stood on the quiet, deserted Doncaster Street and recalled a sex worker who, fifteen years ago, had been stabbed in the neck about eighteen times in a carpark just a few blocks from here. The murder had never been solved. He feared Rita's murder might never be solved either.

Still walking around Fulwood, Joe's phone rang again. It was Sally calling to say that Colin came back to work. Making his way to his car, Joe made his way to the Co-Op store to see him. Waiting by the checkout, he was approached by a chubby young man with glasses and long stringy hair worn back in a ponytail. Colin politely offered his hand to Joe in greeting, and the two stepped outside to have a few words. Yes, he spoke to Rita all the time. She liked him and he couldn't understand why people said she was hard to talk to. He remembers that day when a customer came in wearing a CORP uniform.

"You know, the security guard people. He said Rita became really agitated, saying, 'That's the uniform! The cop! Maybe he's here too. He's coming for me and he will help me get my baby.' She said she wanted her baby and she suddenly started acting as though this guy was just gonna come in the door and bring it to her. But he wasn't a cop, I told her. He was a guard from CORP. She read the name wrong on the uniform. The silly girl could hardly read anyway. If it weren't for the pictures on the labels she'd likely put the tins in the wrong places."

"So she recognized the man?" Joe stroked the stubble on his chin.

"No, she just recognized the uniform. I told her again, she was daft. They were not cops. Then she said she needed to tell her boyfriend."

"I didn't know she had a boyfriend. Who is he?"

"I have no idea who he is, I never asked. Why? Don't you know?"

Joe shook his head. "Could be Sally knows. I'll check with her later."

Colin went on, "And I keep remembering little things that she said. 'I thought they was cops.' Anyway, she said he left her, saying he'd be back. She said he never came back. 'Maybe now he can help me find my baby. I want to know where my baby is. So, if he just goes and tells 'em what happened…' she used to say."

Joe could not even imagine the girl's anguish.

Colin continued, "But I kept telling her that it doesn't work that way. They ain't just gonna give you your baby because some bloke says he done it. And he won't come back, Rita. She said he left her, but I didn't understand what that meant, if she didn't even know his name. The more we talked, it sounded like this guy might have raped her. So I asked her that."

Colin was whispering now. "Rita said to me, 'Yes I think I know that now. I didn't know then, but still he should have to pay. He promised he would come back. I'd rather die than not know where my baby is.' But the truth was, she didn't even know who he was."

"Can you do me a favour Colin? Can you go get Sally and meet me back here?"

Colin went to find Sally, and Joe stayed outside by the bench that was located to the side of the door. When Colin returned with Sally, Joe asked her,

"I'm very curious about this boyfriend, Sal. Do you know anything about him?"

Sally looked up at Joe and said, "No, Joe. Like I said, she wasn't exactly friendly. We never saw anyone around the store, and she never talked to anyone but Colin."

"I hate to ask you this, but could you ask around to your co-workers over the next few days? Maybe we could get a description from someone? Better I didn't hang around doing it; your boss likely wouldn't be too happy about it."

"Sure thing. And Joe, about that other girl, Mary. She's not here, but I asked her about the day Rita said she recognized someone. She said she doesn't remember anything else about it. She says Colin was there and had the same information."

"Thanks, Sal, you've been helpful and I appreciate it."

Sally smiled as she headed back inside.

So it seemed nobody knew who Rita's boyfriend was, only that she had one. Why didn't anyone tell Joe sooner?

Something else was bothering Joe. "Colin, do you know why Rita would not have acted on this a long time ago?"

"I dunno, but maybe it's because Rita had gone away for a long time and had only been in Sheffield for these last six months or so. Maybe she hadn't seen any CORP uniforms until now. Maybe there were none where she was living before. She acted really alarmed when she saw it. I mean, it was like she saw a ghost. I guess it brought back memories or something."

"Can you remember anything else, Colin? What about what you and this Mary girl heard?"

"Yes. Rita said she saw a man at Banner Cross, coming out of a bakery. Just a few days before she was murdered. She said he didn't remember her but she remembered him. She was sure of it. So she followed him to Tesco's, where she confronted him in the parking lot. Apparently he told her to sod off, saying she was out of her mind and had the wrong bloke. She threatened to tell everyone if he didn't give her money to help her find her baby."

"She said that, did she? It seems an odd thing to say," Joe considered. His stomach was growling. What was it with him lately? He couldn't recall being this hungry so often.

Joe thanked Colin and gave him his contact information, asking him to please call if he remembered anything else, or if he was able to find out just who this boyfriend was. Joe then headed to Tesco's.

CHAPTER 37

Joe arrived at Tesco's, which was only a short distance away. Taking a chance, he went in with Rita's photograph to ask if anyone was here last month and witnessed the incident. He would have preferred to have a photograph of a living Rita with her eyes open, but the morgue photo would have to do. After inquiring with every employee he came upon, he eventually found someone who did remember. One of the cashiers was just starting her shift when she saw the two of them in parking lot.

"I thought it was a girl arguing with her father. She looked pretty frantic, and he sounded angry."

"Do you remember what the man looked like?" asked Joe.

"Not really, it weren't important I suppose. He was tall, white."

"Like half of Sheffield," Joe thought to himself.

So this was putting a whole different spin on things. There was no cop involved. Joe would need to go to CORP and have a talk with them. He kicked himself for not going last week when he had first thought about it.

It would be important for Joe to find the person who was dispatched that night in November 2007 when Rita was found in the front entranceway. That person might hold the key to this mystery. He thanked the woman for her help and got into his car, heading across town to CORP. Joe had a funny feeling in his stomach as he approached the building. It seemed another lifetime ago since he was there last. His recollections of those days were not good ones.

For the first time, he parked in the visitor's section and headed across the expansive parking lot. He walked into the reception area in hope that Simon's first wife Eva still worked there. He smiled at the receptionist, a young girl with mousy brown hair rolled up in a knot on top of her head.

"How can I help you, sir?" she asked, with a smile that displayed a mouth full of braces.

"Can you help me please? I'm trying to contact Eva Fisher. Can you tell me if she still works here?"

"I'm sorry I don't know that name," the girl answered apologetically.

Just at that moment, one of the supervisors saw Joe in the hall and recognized him.

Walking over, she called out, "Is that you, Joe Parrott?" Looking over at the receptionist, she called out, "It's okay, Connie, I've got this."

Joe didn't recognize the woman but said nothing. He needed her help. She invited Joe to an interior waiting area. The room was dimly lit with very modern décor. On the wall was an oversized painting that Joe recognized as one by Didier Lourenco. It was named "Red Jazz". It also happened to be the only Lourenco that he knew by name. Looking at it made him think of Aisha. Looking away and focusing, he told the woman his reason for being there.

After listening, the woman told Joe that he needed to go and speak with dispatch. Directing him to the operations area of the building, she wished him good day and went on her way. She seemed unconcerned whether or not he knew who she was.

Joe walked down the corridor, which was sterile looking with its white walls and pale grey floor. Much different than the way he remembered it. Every face was strange and the place seemed much smaller. Approaching the dispatch room, he knocked on the open doorframe. Another young new face motioned for him to come in. All these young faces were making Joe feel very old.

"I need to send someone into the vault to get the old log books. Can I call you?"

"Yes, that would be helpful. So I am guessing no database?"

"Well, yes, we have one now, but I think it was created about five years ago so it would not have the old logs on it. New system, you know. The plan was to start current."

"Okay, brilliant. If I leave you with my card, can you call me when you find it?"

"Sure thing, Mr. Parrott," replied the young man, reading Joe's name on the card. "Hey, is that really your name? Parrott?"

Joe grimaced a smile at him and said nothing as he turned and left.

He didn't have to wait long. Joe received a call two days later.

"Hi, Mr. Parrott. I got the record. The fellow who responded to the call was a fellow named Gary Whitely. I checked our employment records, and he doesn't work here anymore. The bloke retired a few years back. Then I checked with our personnel department, and their records show he moved to Castleton. I don't have any contact information for him."

"I think I can find it, thanks again for the information."

Joe hung up the phone. He hadn't been to Castleton for some time. His memory took him back to his childhood, to the time his uncle came for a visit from the U.S. with his family. His cousins were a few years younger than him. He had disliked them right away, finding them spoiled and disinterested in everything. His parents had planned a trip to the caves to see the Blue John stone.

The caves themselves were massive. They were deep, damp and cold. His cousins had been initially interested when they heard that Blue John is a semi-precious mineral that is found only in these caves. The mineral deposits themselves are about 250 million years old. But their enthusiasm waned once they were inside the cold mammoth caverns.

Joe's uncle and his father, Ivan, had both been cops in Washington State. His uncle had by now worked his way up in the ranks, while Ivan had become a sheep farmer. They were both tough men. So Joe found it very odd that upon entering the caves, his cousins became frightened. The boys started to cry. Joe was uncomfortable the whole time. He had expected more resilience from his companions. They were not permitted to go back, only forward, so needed to endure the tour.

Many years later, both his cousins had become police-men as well, and ironically, the eldest son, Steve had later become a Private Investigator, same as Joe. Thinking back, he found it amusing that two such wimpy kids finished up as cops.

Tourists would flock to the caves to buy jewelry made from the beautiful blue stone. His aunt bought a bag full of earrings and bracelets to take back to the USA. During tourist season the miners work as guides, leading public groups through the caverns. Joe remembers his school class doing the tour when he was fourteen years old. Their teacher had a bad fall in the caves. Certain areas inside the caverns are hard to negotiate. One particular section has a flight of stairs with over ninety steps. Their teacher fell down the last twenty. As well as steep and uneven, they were slippery with water. Fortunately he wasn't badly hurt.

It wasn't difficult finding Gary Whitely. A phone call was all it took for Joe to find out where he was. With hardly a thought about it, Joe grabbed his coat and drove to Castleton.

Gary had a little booth on the edge of the road by his cottage where he sold honey. "Blossom honey and heather honey. It's the finest around and the locals love it," the man boasted. Joe bought a few jars.

"Do you remember that day, Glen?" he asked as he took the glass honey jars.

"Sure, I remember. But I wasn't the first person dis-patched. I got a call over the radio from that weird bloke. I can't remember his name right now. He said he couldn't take the callout, as he was too far away, and could I please not say anything about it. So I went, I was near enough. I found the girl nearly passed out. I'm no doctor, but I'd swear she was delirious with fever. Her teeth were chattering from the cold. It was raining and she was wet. I can't remember his name, but he was a tall bloke.

Joe was aware of how short Glen was, and imagined everyone was tall to him. "Did you write that in your report? CORP said it was you that was dispatched."

"I changed the log and put my name in. He asked me not to log it, we patrollers cover for each other like that," was Glen's reply.

"So were you complicit? You purposely covered for him not going?"

"It weren't a big deal," said Gary. "Dispatch called the cops, and they took it from there."

"Did you talk to the girl at all? Ask her if she was okay?"

"She just kept saying, "No, no." Had her hands up over her face, defensive like. As I said, I think she was delirious."

Joe was angry. This man covered for someone. If he went back to CORP would they possibly have record of who was called first? Joe would need to investigate that possibility.

Driving away, he looked at his gas gauge. He would need to stop for petrol. As he pulled into the roundabout two big lorries sped by him. His thoughts took him to Aisha's husband and daughter the day they were killed and she was left standing by the side of the road. Living through something like that would require a lot of strength, which he had no doubt Aisha had developed.

CHAPTER 38

Joe was still thinking about his trip to Castleton as he checked his mailbox. In the box lay one plain brown envelope. Picking it up, he turned around and headed back indoors. He was still pissed off at Glen Whitely. Firstly, for not recording the dispatch properly and secondly, for not remembering the guy's name.

He tore open the envelope to read the contents. The DNA test results came back positive. Stefan was without a doubt Aidan's uncle. Joe went into the front room, feeling pleased, and headed to the phone. He first called Stefan and left a message. His next call was to the Dwights to ask if they had also received the news. Lastly, he called DI Wilkes. The DNA results could now be used to check databases. With any luck, there was a match out there somewhere for Aidan's biological father.

"We'll get on it, Joe. But keep in mind, this doesn't mean the father is in our database. We don't have every man in the bleeding country in there."

Joe was aware but tried not to think of it.

Liam Dwight called Joe a day later to say that he and his wife have decided to proceed with a Skype call with Stefan.

"We have friends who look at us like we are crazy, and other friends that think we are right on target. Can't please everyone, but we both feel good about it. It's our boy and we want the best for him."

"That's great, Liam. Tell me what you want and I'll set it up."

They picked a day and time, leaving the details for Joe to look after.

"By the way, Joe, you mentioned that you are working on behalf of Stefan. I'm curious, how is that young man paying you?"

"He's actually not paying me. It's a long story. I'm working on his behalf but not specifically for him. Besides, I think he's okay now. All he wanted was to find you."

Joe had spoken with Stefan earlier, when he had given him the good news about the DNA. The lad was beside himself. Imagine how he will react when he hears this news as well.

The phone rang only twice before Stefan answered. "Hi Stefan? I have some news for you."

The Dwights set the meeting up for Wednesday morning. Stefan would call from Joe's office, as he had a big computer screen. Joe was now in the office waiting for the lad to arrive. Everything was set up as per Mr. Harvey's instruction. The click of the front door opening and closing, and the murmuring in the front office let Joe know that Stefan had arrived. He walked into Joe's office, a look of anxiousness on his face. "I'm okay, but I've got butterflies. I'm all fidgety. What if they don't like me?"

"Just be yourself, Stefan. You'll do fine. This isn't a judgment session. You are under no scrutiny."

Once Stefan had settled into his chair, Joe dialed the number, then handed the phone to Stefan. He stayed in the room but moved out of the line of vision, on the other side of the desk. After the initial introductions, Stefan's essence began to reveal itself. It was a warm conversation, the Dwights telling Stefan that they were eagerly waiting for him to meet their son. Hopefully in time he would become a part of the family. Aidan would have a real uncle. They asked Stefan if he was aware of any health history in the family. Stefan said he would speak with his mom. He then told them about his mom's cancer.

Stefan went from tense to relaxed in a short space of time. Joe had no doubt that Elaine and Liam would be quick to take a liking to him. Stefan was unaware of his own appeal. He had plenty. That was one of the nice things about him. His remarks could be precipitous and bold, but he was honest and likeable. You could count on Stefan to speak his mind.

Joe also knew that Elaine would warm to his honesty and approachability. Throughout the conversation her words were kind. Elaine eventually spoke about Aidan.

"Aidan looks very much like you do, Stefan. I am thrilled at the idea of having a real blood uncle to tell him about. Our original plan was to wait until he turns sixteen before we tell him he was adopted. And at that time we would tell him about you. But Liam and I have now agreed that we will do it sooner than sixteen. But we do want to wait another year or two before that happens. We will discuss it again and let you know. I realize this will be difficult for you but our first concern is our son."

Liam added, "We'll have you come around soon, to meet him. But we will wait to tell him who you are. I hope you understand this has been an overwhelming turn of events for us. We don't want Aidan to be overwhelmed as well, with things he may not yet fully understand."

Stefan fought back tears as he said, "I think Aidan is lucky to have you. I'd rather be adopted by strangers who are going to love me and give me a fighting chance, than be raised by parents who treat you like shit and take all your chances away from you."

"That was well said, Stefan. Thank you," said Elaine.

"Blood matters, and with you being our son's only relative, it will be so important for him to know you," added Liam. "And you can tell us all about his mother."

"Well, I can tell you what I know, but I'm afraid it's not much," he cautioned.

When Stefan hung up the phone he leaned forward in his chair, his head resting on his arms. His body was wracked with tremors. He was crying. Joe left the room to give the lad a moment to himself, before he would get him out of the office to a better environment.

"Sit down. I'll grab us a couple of pints." Joe and Stefan had decided on the Norfolk Arms for their meal.

Stefan stopped him. "No, wait. Do you think I could have something stronger today? I think I need it."

They both had a gin and tonic, followed by a pint with their fish and chips. After they ate, they sat at length, not always talking but musing in their own heads. Joe sensed a calmness slowly start to flow from Stefan. They sat at length doing little more than people watch. After a while Joe was the first to speak.

"Are you sure you won't stop over? It's a long drive back."

Stefan smiled. "No, it's good. I actually really enjoy the drive and it helps me clear my head. Plus I always have good tunes to listen to. I'll see you later Joe, and thanks again."

Late that evening as Joe was turning out the lights, he received a text from Liam Dwight. "Are you still up? Can I call you?"

To which Joe answered, "I'm here if you want to call."

Within seconds the phone rang. "You mentioned that you are working pro bono for the young man. There's still the issue of the murderer and who the father is. Will you still go ahead with that?"

"I likely will, because that's what I do. I haven't yet discussed it with Stefan."

"What I am about to propose may sound a bit unusual to you. I know this is unorthodox to say the least, but my wife and I have had a long talk about it. What I mean is, we will pay you. We want to help see this thing through. He wants to know what happened to his sister. He seems a determined young man. So we will hire you and cover any costs going forward, Joe. May I call you Joe?"

Liam had Joe's full attention. "I do want to find the killer. Maybe now more than ever." He spoke with more enthusiasm than he intended.

"That's bloody brilliant," was Liam's reply. "I will have my lawyer draw up a contract if you can give me the name of your agency. Thank you, Mr. Parrott. I mean Joe." Liam sounded as enthusiastic as Joe.

CHAPTER 39

A good part of Thursday was spent with his dad. Joe had driven to the hospital to take Ivan home. Earlier that morning, the doctor had discharged him with a clean bill of health. The instructions were to drink less coffee and take more walks. Joe's mom agreed to take care of these two issues.

Neighbour Rob came to Joe's door and peered inside. Joe was bent over, having arrived home late, and was just removing his jacket and boots. Rob's voice from behind made him jump.

"Eh up, Joe. 'Ow do?" said Rob.

" 'Ow do, Rob. Strange to see you here this late."

"Well, I've been waiting for you to come home. You see, my dog found a knife on the road," he said as he handed the knife to Joe. It was wrapped in a piece of newspaper. Joe carefully unwrapped the package and looked at the knife. It had a shiny blue patterned handle.

"I was going to pass it on to police, but I thought it might have something to do with your girl. Someone might have dropped it, but how many people lose their knives with the blade open?"

Joe looked at it closely to see the logo. The label identified it as a Spyderco.

"Funny thing is, I saw someone here, by your door. I tried to get a better look, but by then, he walked away down the street. All the way, down that side," he said, pointing. "See, it was right past there, where my dog found the knife." He looked at Joe's humourless expression. "I meant funny strange, not funny funny," he clarified.

"When was that, Rob?"

"I think it was the night the girl was killed."

"And you are only telling me now?" questioned Joe.

"You are not an easy man to talk to. Joe. A person might think you were avoiding them." The man raised his voice in defense. "And until I found the knife, I thought it was someone calling at your door to see you. How was I to know there might be a connection?"

"I'm sorry, Rob, you are right," Joe said with some embarrassment. His evasion technique had not been as subtly cunning as he had hoped. Joe was upset as he took the knife and re-wrapped it in the newspaper. "Of course, you didn't know. But thanks, mate, thanks for bringing it to me. I owe you one," he responded kindly as he placed his hand on Rob's shoulder.

After Rob left, Joe called the police station to try to reach Harry or David. Within an hour, two officers arrived at Joe's. He pointed them to Rob's home, where they could see Rob waiting on his doorstep. Giving a wave, he walked towards the officers. Joe left them to it, as his neighbour showed them the exact spot where the knife was found. This discovery was profoundly disturbing to Joe.

His thoughts turned to Stefan, which had been happening a lot lately. The meeting with the Dwights went as good as could be expected. The call from Liam was well timed as well, as Joe didn't exactly have cases lined up and he had bills that would need to be paid. Although it was usually Stefan who was calling Joe, he picked up his phone and sent him a text. Before long, his phone rang. It was Stefan.

"I'm in London, Joe. With me mum, and me aunt. We've been going through Rita's things. I don't know why I didn't do it sooner. She's got a picture of you, Joe. It's a newspaper clipping, from your accident in the stairwell. I found the clipping between the pages of a book. I almost missed it. Why would she have that?"

Rita had his picture. Why the hell would she want that? So she was not on his street by some strange chance. She had meant to be there.

"Hey Joe, she had some other stuff as well, like a few books on turtles. And here's something else, Joe. At the bottom of one page she's got the letters AK, and the words Andrew King written inside a heart with kisses. Actually, it's all over the place on bits of paper."

Joe sat up. "Andrew King."

"Joe, that name Andrew King. Isn't that the name of that man from the Nether Edge Hotel? Could he be the son? Isn't that where she worked? That man might have a son. Maybe the man was lying saying he didn't know anyone who knew Rita." Stefan was tripping over his words in excitement. He sensed something in Joe's voice.

For a split second Joe felt baffled. That could be why Thomas was acting so cagey. But this was going against his new theory.

"Well, the man seemed to be holding something back, you said so yourself," Stefan said excitedly.

"I'll have a look at her things when you get back, Stefan, and we can go from there. Thanks for the call." He ended the call and immediately dialed the number for the Nether Edge. It went to voicemail. He left a message.

"Thomas, I'm coming over tomorrow. This time, no more pissing about. You need to tell me about Andrew and Rita. I'd come now if it weren't so late."

Joe hung up and went to lose himself in front of the TV screen.

Early the following morning Joe was awakened by the sound of vehicles on the street. The police had begun a wider sweep of the area. After quickly getting himself ready, Joe went to his office to get out of the way, plagued by nagging theories about the knife and now someone named Andrew King. Unable to concentrate on anything, he called to inquire again about the DNA results. There was still no match.

His next call was to Thomas King. The man picked up on the second ring.

"Thomas, where is Andrew?" He berated the man. "He is your son, right? The one you neglected to mention?"

Thomas bit back defensively. "You'll not accuse my boy, he's done nothing wrong."

"Is this why you have been keeping him from me? From the police? You thought we'd accuse him? What were you thinking, man? He knows something, and we need to talk to him. Do you realize the trouble you could get into for obstructing justice like this?"

"He didn't do it. He were out looking for her that night. He said he needed to find the man in the paper, as that was where Rita was headed. It was late in the afternoon and she'd gone off in a frenzy."

"I'm on my way over, Thomas."

"I'm not at the hotel right now. I'm out of town. I should be back in the morning, Mr. Parrott. I will call you when I get there, I will." With that, the man promptly cut the line.

Joe looked around the room for something to throw. His frustration was growing.

Eventually, he headed back home unsure what he should do next. He had a lot going on in his mind, thinking back hard, to times and dates, trying to remember certain events as they happened. He had an uncomfortable feeling at the pit of his stomach and a very bad taste in his mouth. Still, he was sure he had the mystery solved. He was just reluctant to admit it.

While driving down Fulwood Road, he pulled over and called Simon. Liz answered the phone, telling him that Simon was not home.

"How are you, Liz? How's Simon?

"I don't know what's up with that man, Joe. He has seemed distracted, not himself. I know he says it's because of my daughter, but sometimes I'm not so sure. Maybe this moving in thing is not what he really wants. He's been off the rails for the last month."

"Where is Simon now?" Joe asked.

"He's out on a job. He shouldn't be gone much longer. I'm just on my way to my daughter's."

"Can you do me a favour? Can you stay at your daughter's until I call you on your cell? I need to come and talk to Simon about something, and I need to do it alone."

"What's wrong, Joe?"

"It's likely nothing. I need to pick his brain about something he might remember." Liz seemed to be waiting for more of an explanation so he added, "Someone may have been looking for him, trying to find information about a guy we might have known when we worked for CORP." Joe had already turned his car around, driving towards Simon's.

"Okay," Liz replied.

Joe's phone rang again almost immediately after he hung up. He grabbed it off the seat. Thinking it was Simon, he answered, "Hey, are you on your way home?"

He was surprised by a deep voice. "It's Harry, Joe. They found the bike, over in Storth Park. The boys are taking in to the station now. The bike and the knife will be dusted for prints, and we'll test the blood to see if we can get a match."

"Thanks for the update, Harry. Let me know when you have something." Joe had arrived at Simon's and was parked in front of the house. While he sat there, his mind wandered. He found himself thinking of the dimple on Aisha's right cheek.

Checking his watch he realized he'd been there for over half an hour. Simon never came home. He picked up the phone and called Liz, letting her know that Simon hadn't come, and that she can come home when she was ready. Funny thing is, just as he was speaking to her, he could have sworn he saw Simon's car in the rear-view mirror driving towards the house. But when he glanced back again, the car was gone.

He tried Simon's cell, but again, there was no answer. It went straight to voicemail. All of a sudden, he had a new plan. Joe left a message before he turned around and headed home.

Joe got out of the shower and grabbed the towel from the hook. He didn't want to be at home for very long; he just needed a scrub and a bite to eat. His phone rang just as he was reaching for his trousers. It was David calling to say the blood on the knife matched Rita's. There was no match yet on the prints.

"You don't sound surprised," said Harry. "Actually, it sounds like you know what I am going to say before I say it. Why do I get the feeling you know something that I don't?" Harry probed. He must have sensed the delay in Joe's response.

"It might be nothing, Harry. Just a hunch I have."

Wilkes scolded Joe, "You do know something, don't you? Don't you withhold shit from me Joe."

"Just give me a couple of hours, Harry, that's all."

Joe hung up the phone. Grabbing his car keys, he headed for the door.

CHAPTER 40

Joe drove to Nonna's in search of Simon. There was still no answer on his cell but he had a good idea where to find him. His next stop would be the Nether Edge Hotel to have a harsh word with Thomas King. He knew he was taking a chance that Thomas had returned, but he needed to know more about Andrew and how he fit into this puzzle.

He was now driving down Sharrow Vale Road, having been unsuccessful at finding parking on Ecclesall Road. Sure enough, as his car approached the chip shop, Joe spotted Simon parking his car. He pulled up behind him a little too quickly, slamming on his brakes, tires squealing as he avoided ramming into the back of Simon's car.

"What are you doing here, Joe?"

As Simon spoke, Joe caught the noticeable smell of liquor on his breath. "I just want to talk to you, Simon. Where've you been? I've been around to see you. Didn't Liz tell you?"

"She didn't say. What do you want, man?" There was something different about Simon's demeanour.

"I just want to talk to you," he said with a deep breath.

"Why the sudden interest in me, Joe? You've been preoccupied from what I can tell. So why now?" was his caustic reply.

"Where's your fishing knife, Simon?"

"Why do you want to know?"

"Found one near my house."

"It's not mine."

"Blue Spyderco, Simon. Not many of those around. Not many trout fishermen in my neighbourhood."

"Don't look at me, Joe. I was nowhere near your place."

"That's where you are wrong, Simon. You were seen there, the night Rita died." Joe felt his face turn red and said, "Show me your knife, man."

"You're not going to throw me to the wolves are you, mate? I just misplaced my knife is all. I must have dropped it when I was there. That's not a crime."

"So, you were there. That brings me to another question. Why were you there? It was late, and you knew I'd gone out to meet you. You don't normally come over equipped with a blade."

"I always have my knife in my pocket, you know that." As if to realize he may have said the wrong thing, Simon sighed and leaned on the hood of the car.

"So show it to me, Joe repeated.

"Don't pull that PI shit with me Joe. Go pick on a real criminal." Simon didn't move.

"You know something, Simon. I can see it in your face, and I want you to tell me."

"Simon kicked at a bit of loose dirt alongside the curb, spun around, and quickly walked away. "Sod this, I'm going to get my coffee."

Joe stood there, momentarily at a loss for words. Still he knew that even with suspicion alone, he needed to tell Wilkes. And Simon needed an alibi, friend or not. Was he covering for someone they knew? What precisely did he know about Rita?

Joe quickened his pace and followed him into Nonna's. He grabbed his arm as hard as he could. He felt Simon wince. "Either you get that coffee to go and come outside with me right now, or I'm going to drop you, right here in front of everyone."

In silence, Simon paid for his coffee. The two men then walked across the street. They carried on up Dover Road to sit in the Botanical Gardens. Joe was trying to read Simon but got nothing. The man was cool.

"Tell me what's up with you, Simon."

"Okay, I did go to your place that night, after fishing. I thought you might still be home. I guess I must have dropped my knife there. Surely anybody could have picked it up."

"You told me you missed the football match because you and Vincent were late getting back, Simon." Joe's blood was starting to boil. This was becoming disturbingly bothersome. "It has Rita's blood on it, Simon."

"Well, that's got nothing to do with me, does it? Someone else likely found it and used it."

"Okay, then you won't mind coming to the police station and offering your fingerprints to clear you."

"What are you trying to do, arrest me?"

"You know I can't do that, Simon. I'm just trying to make sure no one else tries. Let's clear this up before that happens."

Simon sat in silence. Joe had no idea what he should do.

"You are lying to me, Simon. And it will come out because I won't let this go."

Slowly, Simon got up to walk away. Joe grabbed his arm and told him to start talking. He felt his hand form into a fist.

Simon lowered himself in resignation and began speaking. "Okay, fine. I had first seen the girl a few weeks ago, when I was in the Co-Op store. She came running out after me, yattering on about how she knew me, how she needed my help. I walked away as quick as I could. I thought she was on drugs. Then I was at Tesco two days later when this same girl runs out after me and starts yelling, 'You.' She was pointing right at me. People were staring. I didn't know what she were on about."

Both Simon and Joe seemed to calm down a bit at this point. Simon was somehow getting the words out, and Joe was afraid to interrupt him.

"So, she starts following me after that. She even hid out in the ginnel on Psalter Lane to wait for me to pass. She was on about a uniform and a baby. I kept walking away. Actually running away. I had no idea what she were on about."

"I think she might have wanted your help to find someone, Simon. Someone from CORP. Maybe she saw you with someone who she was trying to find. I think someone from there may know something about her baby, and she was looking for help."

"I don't know anything about that, but she was becoming crazy. I was on my way to your place after fishing, driving along Fulwood Road. I saw her standing in front of your house. I drove past her to park. We argued. I got pissed off and I just wanted her to shut up. I didn't mean it, she just made me mad."

"What did you argue about?"

"I don't know, she were just yelling at me. The words didn't make sense. She said she was going to tell you, and tell my girlfriend. She said she'd make me suffer if I didn't help her."

"Wanted you to help her how?"

"She wanted money. Why should I give her money? She said that you and me would pay. Then she came at me like a sodding wolverine! I had to defend myself."

"Defend yourself? She was a wee spit of a girl."

"She was threatening me. I wasn't about to bend over for some skirt who tries to threaten me. She got me mixed up with someone else. She's just some cheap little blackmailer. I think too much of myself."

"Was she armed? Did you feel in any danger?" Joe was yelling.

"Stop cross examining me, Joe, I felt threatened."

"So killing her is the answer?"

"Yes, sorry, I killed her. Yes, I slit her, like a fish, to shut her up. Is that what you want me to say?"

"So that's why you didn't come to the pub that night?"

"I guess I lost the mood at that point," was all Simon could say.

"I don't have the vocabulary to say what I want to say to you, Simon. You know I have to tell the police." Joe was spitting the words.

"No, you don't need to do anything Joe. This is me! Besides, who's to know? It's all over now. You'll not tell, Joe. It's me, man."

"You are my mate, Simon. But the truth is all I want to hear right now. I won't cover for you. All the girl wanted was some help to find her baby. She could be alive right now, and she could be with her brother, and she could know her baby is safe. But you've taken that away from her."

"What do you want me to say? I panicked."

"But yet you carefully hid her bike?"

"That weren't me who did that." Simon's leg was jerking and he was sweating.

"Sure it wasn't, Simon." Joe said sarcastically as he stood up. He needed some quick distance between them. Simon's disposition had changed and he was becoming unhinged. Joe wanted very badly to hit him.

CHAPTER 41

"I won't confess, Joe. I'll deny everything. Liz will give me an alibi. You can't prove shit!" Simon yelled after Joe as he was walking away. "Sod you, Joe. Sod you and sod your new boyfriend."

Joe shook his head. He was disturbed at the level of antipathy he was feeling for his friend. Walking quickly, Simon's voice faded behind him. Taking his phone out of his pocket, he called DI Wilkes. "I need you to come and arrest my best mate, Harry."

"What's going on, Joe?"

"He has involvement in the death of Rita. Actually, he just confessed to killing her. He says he'll deny it, but I think we can prove it. I also have a witness."

"Where are you now? Is he with you?"

"He's here at the top of Dover Road. I don't think he will go far. His car is behind Nonna's on Sharrow Vale Road."

"You better be right about this. I can't just go over and arrest the man."

"He confessed, Harry! You have enough to bring him in for questioning. If he resists, bring him in for suspicion of murder. Or at least for resisting arrest. You will need to get his prints and DNA sample. It's the only way to prove it."

"Thanks Joe, we'll be there."

Wilkes had sent two police officers to wait by Simon's car. Joe watched from across the street, surprised at how quickly they got there. Simon had just reached his vehicle when he saw the squad cars pull up. Joe was sure to stand where Simon could see him.

He knew that Wilkes was putting a lot of faith in him. He would be pissed if it finished up being baseless. Simon pushed past the officer and defiantly unlocked his car door, trying to get inside. When the officer took a step towards him, Simon looked like he wanted to run. The sergeant in charge asked Simon to calm down. Joe winced, as he knew what would happen if anyone asked him to calm down.

It was then that Simon lost it. He threw his arms in the air, both hands rolled into fists. He was swearing, passersby stopped to see what was going on. He opened his car door and was half way inside when the officer shouted at him to freeze. Stepping forward quickly, the officer pulled out his handcuffs and cuffed him. Resisting, Simon was pushed into the squad car, hollering profanities at Joe.

Once Simon was in the car and it had driven away, Joe went to the sergeant and asked, "So what will happen now?"

Well, DI Wilkes will talk to him and hopefully we can formally arrest him, like you said, on suspicion of murder. I don't know how much more can be done until we get some real evidence. You'd better come along and tell us what's going on. We can only question him at this point. And, Joe, we may not be able to hold him."

"I'll be there, thanks. But I have to make one stop first," was Joe's answer. He got into his car and drove the short distance to see Liz. His head was in a black fog. He still couldn't figure out why Simon would have done what he did.

Liz sat down, her face flushed at the news. "I think I might faint," she said. "What a piece of shit. And I've been sleeping with him."

Joe went to the kitchen and brought her a glass of water. The house was eerily quiet. "Can we go sit outside?" asked Joe.

They moved outside to the stoop. The air was deathly still. It was as if time had stopped.

"Well at least this explains Simon's erratic behaviour lately. It probably had nothing to do with my daughter." Liz sat on the front step beside Joe.

"Liz, do you remember that afternoon? I know he had gone fishing with Vincent. Do you remember what time he got home?"

"I can ask Vincent what time he dropped him off. He's the best person to ask. I can't remember because I might not have been here."

"Let me know when you find out, can you love?" inquired Joe.

"I will, Joe. But please don't go just yet. Can you sit with me here a minute?"

Sitting there, Joe felt tense but not awkward. He had known Liz a long time. This would have a significant impact on her, and Joe was certain she was thinking about what her daughter would say.

He was going over different scenarios in his head. So maybe Rita thought Simon was someone else? The man did have a temper, and anyone who knew him well knew that. But this was not like him. What drove him to kill the girl? She attacked him, he said, but she was small. She had no weapon. When he finally got up to leave, Liz seemed calmer. He still had to go to see Wilkes.

"I really need to go, Liz. Will you be okay then?" he asked her.

"Yes, I'll call my daughter, and she might come over. Otherwise I'll go to her. Thanks again Joe."

Dusk had fallen. Joe arrived to the stillness of his house. He had spent the last hour and a half with Wilkes going over his timelines and theories. Wilkes nodded throughout his statement. When they had concluded, Harry walked him to the door.

"Have a good night, Joe. You've had quite the day."

Joe arrived home not remembering actually driving. Taking his shoes off, he walked through the kitchen into the front room. The only sound was the creaking of the wood floor as he moved across it. But Joe didn't sit in his chair. Instead, he went over to the wall cabinet and opened the big cupboard door on the side. Blowing the layers of dust from the bottle of Bowman's, he poured himself four fingers. He stood there for a moment in the dark stillness, his eyes closed, as he welcomed the peaty burn of the liquid, willing it to anesthetize his grief.

Then he headed for the thinking chair to sit for a spell before retiring. Something was still very wrong. A nagging thought was why did both Colin and Simon say that Rita had been asking for money? Why was she asking Simon for money?

CHAPTER 42

In the distance, Joe heard screeching tires and the honking of horns. It was still dark outside. The chaos wouldn't have woken Joe, though, as he had hardly slept. He was lying in bed waking up when his phone rang. It was Stefan calling to say that he'd just returned from London visiting his mom.

"And, Joe," he added, "my mum doesn't know anything about my dad. She has no idea where he might be. She said he might not even be alive any more, but a friend says he may have gone back to Poland. She's thrown away every trace of him, not long after he left. So there's nothing I can bring you."

"Stefan, I need to tell you something. We have just arrested a murder suspect."

"Joe, man! That's bloody fantastic! Was it Andrew King? What happened?"

"Stefan, it's my mate Simon."

The line went quiet. I don't think I understand.

"I think she needed to talk to me, and maybe to Simon for some reason. That might be why she was near my house. It could be Simon knew someone who worked for CORP back then. Maybe it was that someone who Rita was looking for."

"So then why would he kill her?"

"I dunno, man. That's what I want to know. Maybe Simon was protecting that person? His reasons for killing her were vague at best."

"So you spoke with him then?"

"It was me who had him arrested, Stefan."

"I'm coming to town tomorrow, Joe. I want to show you these things of Rita's anyway."

"How is your mum?"

"Well, I didn't tell her about Aidan. I wasn't sure what to do. I don't want her to think there might be a chance that she will see him. It'll likely never happen. Mum's in a bad way, Joe. My aunt says she's not got long. Don't know what the right thing is here."

"I'm sorry to hear that, Stefan. Let's talk when you come," was Joe's reply.

He sat at his table eating a piece of toast, a tinge of loss permeating his body. He thought about his conversation with Stefan and was no longer sure how valuable the papers were. Simon had senselessly killed her, for reasons he may or may not have had. It might never be discovered exactly what she had been looking for.

Joe called to get an update on Simon. Now that he had been arrested they would need to find evidence within forty-eight hours or let him go. They had taken blood samples, fingerprints and DNA to see if there was a match with the blood and fingerprints on the knife and the bicycle.

After his breakfast, Joe drove to the police station, having to pass Nonna's on the way. He was paralyzed with disbelief. There would be no more meeting Simon here.

"What are you doing here, Joe?" asked David. "It's too soon to have any results. We will let you know as soon as we do."

Needing something to do, he drove over to Susan's clinic. Maybe she wasn't too busy to have a chat. When he arrived the waiting room was full of pet owners with little animals in their arms or sitting beside their chairs. Without bothering Susan, he left.

Joe felt unbalanced. He needed to do something that would bring him back to reality. He decided he would drive to the farm and visit his dad, who was recovering well enough now that he was back at home. He found his dad and George sitting in the kitchen having tea.

"Sit down, Joe. Want a cuppa?"

"No thanks, Dad. I just came to say hullo. I'll not stay." They obviously had not heard any news yet. He would wait until it was confirmed.

"Nigel is with the young lambs, inoculating them," said George. "Says he will dock some but not all. Sit down, man."

Acquiescing, Joe pulled up a chair. His mum brought him a cup and kissed the top of his head.

"I'm off to see Olivia, so I'll leave you boys to it. We're doing some baking today." She was gone in a flash, likely in need of some woman time, away from the blokes.

It was good to sit with his dad and George for a while. The two were at it again, laughing and crying. The old jokes never got stale. Joe felt himself smile. His shoulders dropped as he began to breathe more calmly. Suddenly he wasn't in a hurry to leave.

It was still light when Joe said goodbye to the two men. On the way home, he stopped at Fox House, feeling somewhat guilty. Carole was outside, getting into a car just as Joe pulled up. It was the same bloke that he had seen her with, that day in silhouette. Seeing Joe, she said something to her companion before walking over to Joe's car. He rolled down his window.

"Hiya, Joe," she said.

"Hi, Carole," he replied as he looked up at her.

Carole had placed her hands on his car doorsill, inches away from his shoulder. "Joe, we need to talk."

"No, we don't, love. You're good. Go on now," said Joe as he smiled and stroked her fingers. She lowered her hands and stepped back when Joe put the car in reverse. They both smiled that kind of smile when you know what's going on but don't want to speak it out loud. Backing out of the parking spot, he decided this was not a good day.

CHAPTER 43

Stefan was meeting Joe late in the afternoon. He had a few things to do himself that would keep him busy until then. He called Liz to see if she had a chance to speak with Vincent.

"I'm sorry, Joe, I haven't. Can I give you his number? I'm not sure I want to talk to him right now." She almost choked on her words. Joe could hear the agitation in her voice. He wrote down the number, telling her he would leave her alone for the time being. She sounded like she could use some peace for a while.

Joe hadn't spoken to Vincent in a long time. He was the youngest brother of Simon's first wife, Eva. He worked for the city council as a painter. Vincent had always enjoyed the work, which involved painting communal blocks of rental flats and maisonettes. These were rental units owned by the city and were very well maintained, being painted and repaired on a regular basis.

Vincent was a decent, hardworking bloke who loved his wife and children. He married young and had a happy life in Waterthorpe. He himself lived in one of these council houses. His only passion was fly-fishing, which he had first started as a boy, with his grandfather.

Picking up the phone, Joe dialed the number and hoped Vincent would answer. He did.

" 'Ow do, Joe. It's been a while, eh?" Vincent's voice was cheerful.

"How are you man? How is your family?" Joe knew he couldn't dive right in with the questions.

"We're good. Mary is well, and the kids are all grown. Two of 'em's married already and two still at home, but working."

"I need to talk to you about Simon. You and he were out on the Wye not long ago, remember?"

"Aye, maybe a month back or longer."

"Do you remember what time you brought him home? It's really important. He's got himself into some trouble."

"I think it was about three o'clock, Joe. I remember because he was hoping to catch Liz before she went off to her daughter's."

"I hate to ask, Vincent, but if the police ask, can you please come to the station to make a statement?"

"Police? What's the man done? He's not knocked Liz about, has he?"

"Why would you say that? Has he done that before?" Digging a bit further, Joe added, "Do you think he ever knocked Eva about, Vincent?"

"No, I'd have clobbered him if he touched my sister. But the way he talked sometimes, I wondered if he would do it to someone one of these days. He was right pissed off at Liz and her daughter. He could be a right wanker, that Simon. But you know, I felt sorry for him. We didn't talk that much, Joe, all we did was fish. His life was of no real concern to me."

Joe would never argue with that statement. Simon had burned more than a few bridges in his day because of his temper. He was starting to wonder why he had indulged Simon for all these years. It wasn't like him to turn a blind eye to these things. What the hell was wrong with him?

"Okay, so if the police call, would you come in and make a statement? I think he's hurt someone else but we need to prove where he was."

"Of course I would, Joe. My Mary wouldn't take too kindly to me holding anything back from police."

"Good man, Vincent, and thank you."

"You know, he's not been the same since he and Eva split. Something happened to him back then. Eva, she's always felt at fault somehow. I told her that was bollocks. He's the one who should feel responsible. You and Simon were a right pair back then, eh Joe? All into the booze and that."

"Don't remind me, Vincent. That was a lifetime ago. You be well, and thanks. Call if you need anything."

And with that, Joe hung up. He was sure they had gone fishing another day as well, but the only important thing was the timeline for this particular day. He would call David and give him the account of his conversation with Vincent.

Joe's enragement didn't stop at the knowledge that Simon killed Rita. It was more than that. He knew there was a missing piece to the puzzle. He went over and over their conversation. He said she made him mad. Why? And he said she was trying to blackmail him, and that she threatened to tell. What did that mean? He wouldn't dismiss these comments but needed to think about them for a while.

Checking the time, he quickly changed his shirt and left the house. On his way to the pub, he encountered a road block. University students, he guessed, with protest signs. This was becoming too common an occurrence since Sheffield City Council came up with the daft idea of felling healthy street trees. They were protesting not only the loss of these trees, but also the impact it would have on the environment and habitat for local birds and such. To date there had already been many arrests and threats of legal action.

While it was true, some were dying and diseased, this purge was including far too many perfectly healthy trees. Magnificent elms and oaks, hundreds of years old, were being massacred and replaced with young saplings. With over 250 parks, gardens and woodlands in the city, well over four million trees in all, this would forever change the beauty of the streets. He patiently idled until he was motioned to drive through.

Joe had arrived at the Prince of Wales early and had chosen a seat on the lower level, near the back door. Stefan waved across the room as he entered the pub from the front. He looked surprisingly fresh and well rested. Stopping at the bar, he came over to the table, pint in hand. He brought the clippings and all Rita's scrawls. But first, they decided to order a meal. The special of the day was liver and onions. Joe ordered the Welsh Rarebit, Stefan the liver.

Stefan then put the box on the table for Joe to open. Rita had few belongings. Two books on turtles, a journal only partly written in, and an advertisement that was likely torn out of a magazine. The ad was for CORP and the big colourful caption read, "Service you can trust." Joe felt a cold chill run through his body at the irony of that remark.

She also had a small scrapbook with cut out pictures of mothers with their babies, and others of young families. These appeared to be randomly cut from magazines. And there it was, neatly tucked away - the newspaper article naming Joe. It was how she found him.

"I must know something she wanted. Both Simon and I." Joe pushed back his chair and started to stand up. "I'm not waiting another minute for that man to get back to me. Let's go, Stefan."

Trying to swallow his last bit of food, Stefan bounced to his feet. "Where are we going?"

Joe's heart rate increased. "To see Thomas. And I guess you will have to come with me this time, Stefan, but please stay in the car."

CHAPTER 44

Thomas looked sheepish as he watched Joe approach the bar.

"You don't look surprised to see me," uttered Joe.

Shaking his head he announced, "I knew you'd be back at my door."

"It would help us if we could speak to your son, Thomas. We know he didn't do it. We have the killer."

Thomas put his elbows on the bar and held his head, letting out a huge sigh.

"Thank you, thank you. I knew he didn't do anything to the girl. He really cared for her." He gave Joe an address and phone number where he could find Andrew. "He's gone to stay with my brother in Stafford. He's hiding from you."

"I don't need to go and hunt him down, Thomas. Just call and ask him to come back. He can come home. He's not in any trouble but we really need his help," said Joe. "Then please call me when he gets home, Thomas. I mean it, or I'll be back with the police and they'll charge you with obstructing justice. They will charge you, Thomas, not Andrew."

Joe returned to the car where Stefan was waiting. He hoped Thomas would call him tomorrow. He filled Stefan in on what the man had told him.

"Stefan, it's late. Why don't you stay the night? You will likely want to come back in the morning and it's too much driving. It's a big house, I have lots of rooms."

Stefan reluctantly agreed. The weather was threatening rain, and the wind had picked up. It would not be a good night to be on the road.

The turbulent wind blew all night, suggesting they would have a poor sleep. Joe rose early and quietly got dressed. Stefan's door was shut. He was likely still sleeping, and Joe didn't want to wake him. He desperately wanted to go and see David as soon as he could. Leaving the house, he saw Rob and he paused to give the man a wave. Rob smiled and waved back.

David had the report. Joe left the police station after being there only a few minutes. The report confirmed that Simon's prints were the only prints on the knife, along with Rita's blood. How could Simon tell him it wasn't his knife? And his prints were also on Rita's bike. Rob had been in earlier to give his statement, so now an eyewitness could place Simon at the scene on that evening.

Joe returned home where he found Stefan having toast and tea.

"I hope you don't mind. I helped myself," he said, almost apologetically.

"No, you're okay. And it looks like I'm just in time." Joe grabbed a cup and sat down to join him.

Stefan twisted his face into an expression of disbelief. "It's a good thing you have no secrets, Joe. I've searched through every cupboard and nook in this room looking for sugar. Who has no sugar?"

"It's over the stove, in the small metal tin." Joe stood up to retrieve the container. He handed it to Stefan, who heaped a spoonful into his tea.

"Who has sugar in tea?" was Joe's sarcastic rebuttal.

The men bantered like an old married couple. Then the conversation became sporadic as each was absorbed in their particular thoughts. Joe was wondering if Simon's leaving CORP had anything to do with Rita. Something happened back then and he was hell-bent on finding out. The timeline fit. Also, Simon's comments, "She was going to tell you and Liz." What did he mean by that? Tell them what?

As if reading his mind, Stefan suddenly spoke. "Who is that man you saw in Castleton? Call him back and give him Simon's name. See if that's the name he was trying to remember," offered Stefan.

"Glen Whitely. Yes, I will call him. Good man, thanks for that." Joe went to get the man's contact number from his jeans pocket. He called the number, but there was no answer. Joe left a message asking if he would call him back straight away.

It was almost noon by the time Stefan left for the drive back to Leicester.

Eva's brother, Vincent, had called in at the station to sign a statement verifying that Simon had arrived home at three that afternoon. By early afternoon, Simon had been formally charged with the murder of Rita Nowak, based on statements from both Vincent and Rob.

Joe hesitated before calling Aisha. Although she wasn't involved in any of this, he wanted to give her the news. They hadn't spoken since their dinner, so he would first say what a nice time he had.

"Why would he do it?" There was disbelief in her voice.

"Well, Colin at the grocery store said Rita recognized someone. Was it someone Simon knew? Or was it Simon?" mused Joe. "Rita had been meaning 'CORP', not 'cop'. Both Simon and I worked for CORP years ago. We might have known someone there, but how Rita made the connection is beyond me."

"Joe, thank you for calling. It means something to me that you wanted to share this. Will you let me know if you hear more?"

"Aye, I will. I apologize for bothering you."

"Its fine, and it gives me a chance to thank you for the dinner. I had a really good time. It was a very needed break from my life."

"Well, if you ever need another break, would you like to come out for a drive into Castleton? I can show you a great little place to buy honey."

"It's a date then. Let's pick a time."

"We could go Saturday morning," Joe blurted out. He didn't want to miss this unforeseen opportunity. "You're not working then, are you?"

Aisha agreed, and so times were discussed. Once they made their plan it was now time to hang up the phone, which Joe did reluctantly. He could have talked to her for hours. With a warm goodbye, Joe promised to keep her up to date. Saturday couldn't come soon enough.

CHAPTER 45

Joe was called to ARD for the monthly conference. He had been offered a new case by referral. Although happy to have his mind on something else, he felt unconcerned and hoped his apathy wasn't visible. When the agenda items were complete, the discussion turned to Joe's new case. It would involve searching out two men who had been running a scam in Arbourthorne Estates. Posing as insurance agents, they had been involved in selling inexpensive policies to the residents, a lot of whom were elderly.

As if on cue, the door opened and two dapper looking older gentlemen walked into the building. They were shown into the meeting room and introduced themselves to Joe. He ushered them into his office and closed the door. Even though the police were investigating, a group of tenants chose to hire Joe on behalf of all, feeling they might get answers quicker. They had heard from one of their lawyers that Joe had been successful on a similar case some years back. Once he had heard the details from the two men sitting across from him, he felt his spirit slightly lift. This could be a good case, both necessary and very timely.

Joe arrived home early in the afternoon, feeling extremely hungry. He assembled a plate of leftovers from a collection in the fridge and headed outside to sit in the yard. He was about to call Stefan when his phone rang. The lad had beat him to it. "They charged him, Stefan. All the prints matched, and the blood matched." As he spoke the words, Joe once again felt overcome with despondency. He was actually more pissed off at Simon than anything. Still, he felt relief. This was a bittersweet victory for Stefan.

Joe had spoken to Glen Whitely in Castleton, who did confirm the name of Simon Hamilton as the bloke whom he filled in for. He now recalled the conversation.

"So the question is, why didn't Simon take the dispatch? Did he have knowledge of someone who was there before you showed up, Glen? Maybe someone he knew, and was protecting?"

"I wish I could help you. I have no idea what went on before I arrived. Maybe nothing happened. Maybe whatever happened to her took place before she arrived at the building. Could she have been running away from someone?"

"I might try to get it out of Simon. He may be more willing to cooperate at this point. Thanks for your time, Glen."

Joe would try to get in to see Simon. He was determined to find a solution to this enigma.

Thomas called just after seven that evening to say that Andrew had returned home. Joe quickly grabbed his keys and headed for the car. He was definitely speeding as he drove over to see the boy. Andrew was seated in the pub, waiting for him. He looked like a younger version of Thomas, only his hygiene appeared to be considerably better. The boy was in a state.

"I couldn't get Rita to stop talking about this cop who raped her, and she wanted to find her baby." He was shaking badly. "I told her we could have our own bairn but she cried and said she didn't think she could have any more. Says she has never tried to be careful and would have been pregnant by now. She believed she would ever only have one baby and wanted to know if that baby is okay. So I told her I would help. I loved her, you know?"

Thomas brought some glasses of beer over to the table. Joe declined but thanked the man.

"She was planning on going to the hospital to try to track down the baby. I told her not to be daft, they'd tell her nothing there. But then she said she had seen him, and she'd been following him. All of a sudden, there was this face, and she recognized him, and all the memories came back. She said it were meant to be, like, a sign. She said she'd even spoken with him but he pushed her off and told her she was crazy. I went with her to the store, and we spoke with Colin. He told me about the uniform 'CORP', not 'Cop'."

Andrew did have a beer and now took a drink. "Then she came with the clipping of you from the paper. She says she knows who you are, that she's seen you with the cop guy. I guess she meant the CORP guy."

"I suppose you don't know if this guy was wearing his uniform?" pressed Joe.

"Nay, that's the odd thing. He was just in normal clothes, but she just turned around and he was standing there, just a regular bloke, but she instantly recognized him, his face close to hers."

Joe tried to think of who that might be.

"She said she needed to find you and talk to you about this guy."

"But you didn't see anyone else, so you had no idea who it could be?"

"I just know what she said. It was the curly blonde guy, she said. The one with the squeaky shoe."

Joe felt the blood drain out of his face. His hands went instantly clammy, and he rubbed his palms against his trousers. "Did she really say squeaky shoe?"

"Yeah, she did. I think she said it was him that did it."

"That he did it, or that he knew who did it?"

"I can't remember. I thought maybe she said he did it."

Joe stood up quickly, "Thanks, Andrew, I have to go. I'll talk to you later."

Andrew and Thomas looked at Joe in a way that would suggest the man had just lost his mind. He needed to get out of there and into the fresh air. He thought he might throw up.

"What did I say?" asked Andrew.

"No, you've done well. Thank you, it's brilliant. I just have to go." And Joe was gone.

As he drove home, Joe's head was churning like an ocean. He couldn't hear anything.

CHAPTER 46

Joe slept late, feeling no particular desire to get out of bed. The coffee was tasteless, and he had no appetite. He was still angry as he put on his shoes and headed outside. He needed to think about something else. Now walking through Storth Park, he was remembering his last conversation with Stefan.

"In a bad world, it's nice to see something good," the lad had said. "You know, Aisha really is a lovely lady, I really don't know what's wrong with you that you haven't called her again."

Joe had revealed that he had taken her out for dinner, partly due to Stefan's nagging him to do it. "We went for honey one day. But I am not too good with relationships. As you can see, they haven't exactly been working out for me."

"Bollocks! You just haven't found someone yet who is the right fit. I'll bet you were a right Jack-the-Lad in your day. Not like me. But I liked a girl once. I mean I really liked her, you know? Asked her out and all. She said yes but then she didn't show up. I waited long after I should have left. I saw her the next day with her mates and they looked over at me and started laughing. It were humiliating. Might not have been because of who I was, but who my freak family was. I should have known better than to bother with her. But you, Joe, you are a catch."

Joe breathed out a silent laugh and said, "I'm not sure I'm such a catch, Stefan."

"In the abstract, you don't think so. But in reality you are. I'll bet if I read The Book of Joe, it'd be pretty normal. Might even be a worthwhile book to read. You've got a good heart."

Joe said, "I don't think I'd be too proud of that book today."

"Yes, but today won't last forever. That's what you told me once. You will colour your gray soon enough, Joe."

Stefan then changed the subject. "Did you know Aisha played football until she was sixteen? Do you think she might have kicked your ass?"

Smiling as he remembered this last part of the conversation, Joe turned around. Finishing his walk, he went home and tried to focus on other things. Feeling hungry, he decided to make breakfast. Just as he was flipping his eggs, the phone rang. It was Stefan calling to see if he was okay. The revelation about Simon had impacted both men in profound ways. For Stefan, it was closure and a way to move forward. For Joe, it was a new awareness, like seeing after being blind. It would change his life forever.

Stefan said, "What if it's him? What if he's the one that raped Rita?"

"I've thought of that as well. But we would need proof," replied Joe. "There was CCTV but that was years ago so likely no one checked it without any cause to."

"We have both lost something big. Yours might be harder to understand. My irony is that Rita needed to die in order for me to find her. They say our struggles shape us. Well, you and me, I figure we are chiseled."

It was a fruitless day. When wandering the rooms in the house was no longer satisfying, Joe retuned outside to wash the car. Rob walked by with his dog and Joe stopped what he was doing to say hello and have a chat.

That same day, Joe had driven to the police station to have a chat with Wilkes, who after a lengthy conversation agreed to test Simon's DNA against that of Aidan's.

The next day Joe was still waiting for the results. In his gut Joe was afraid he already knew the answer. Wilkes called Joe that evening, just as he's turning on Jeopardy.

"Well, the DNA is a match for the child. Your pal Simon is definitely the father."

The words echo in Joe's ears. It is a match. 'Your pal Simon is definitely the father.' The tosser.

"So what do we do now, Harry? Can you charge him with the rape of a dead girl eight years after it happened?"

"I'm afraid not, Joe. We have no way of ascertaining the deceased victim's mental condition and we have lost any ability to do a proper cross-examination. But he'll never see the light of day on the murder charge."

Not enthused with that answer, Joe added, "But will he make bail?"

"That's up to the judge to grant bail or not. We don't know what the odds are, for him to do a runner, and whether Liz would want him out. But given this new information, it's likely he won't be granted bail."

Thanking Harry, Joe hung up the phone. At least there was little likelihood that Simon would be released. Joe was hanging in a fine balance between anguish and outrage.

Joe didn't know who to call but felt he needed to speak to someone. He chose Janet, as she knew Simon well and had not always approved of his actions. He dialed her number, hoping she would be able to speak to him. After four rings, he was about to hang up when he heard her voice on the line.

"Joe, it's you. What's going on? Is everything okay?"

Speaking to Janet was good, although her words were not exactly comforting. However, she summed it up quite nicely. "You always carried him, you know. You always sank to his lows with him. The help you gave him was never reciprocal. He was never any good for you. He was petulant and needy, and you always excused what he really was. I'm proud of what you did, Joe. You could have turned a blind eye. Even if they eventually caught up with him, you might have reassured yourself it wasn't you who turned him in, but you'd have been complicit."

Joe said nothing.

"And that would have been the end of you as well," she added.

Joe sat quietly, damning Simon to hell.

Early the next morning, Joe drove to the Custody and Crimes Centre near Meadowhall. Calling David, the man had informed him that Simon had been transferred to a holding cell there. Joe's aim was to speak to DI Wilkes. He saw the DI just as he was coming out of the monitor-ing room.

"Please let me go see him, Harry. It's important that I do. I owe it to someone who has been waiting a long time to know what happened to his sister. I can get a confession if you have a camera in there."

"I can't give you an interrogation room, Joe. You are here informally. But yes, it won't hurt anyone if you go in, if you don't mind seeing him in his cell. This has been your case, Joe. You solved it."

Joe was cleared and given a pass. He was looking around while being led through the corridors. This new facility really was state of the art. The old building had needed replacement for some time now. While the cells were newer, he noticed they were still basic with a stone bed, loo and basin. But there would be better access to support services, among other things, such as a cup of coffee or a telephone.

His reason for being here was very disturbing. He was still coming to terms with what Simon did. Walking towards Simon's cell, he could feel his heart race. He didn't want to be here; he hated being here. Finally, the guard stopped and motioned to the door on the left. The guard unlocked the cell, and Joe stepped inside.

CHAPTER 47

Simon was sitting on the floor. His eyes were bloodshot. His face was drained of all colour which heightened the redness of his hair and freckles. His facial expression bore the look of a demented man. His nose was crusted and running. Joe had never seen him look so pathetic. What was odd was that he had absolutely no pity for this disgusting man. He wanted to kick him.

Joe reluctantly sat on the corner of the bed, as far away from Simon as he could. Simon sat looking at him, seeming to hold his breath.

At last, Joe spoke. "We got the DNA results back, Simon. Do you know which results I am talking about?"

"I already know. Isn't that why I am here? The blood on my knife and all?"

"No Simon. The DNA results for Rita's baby. Surely you knew we'd be testing it."

"I don't know what you are talking about. It's not my kid, I didn't even know her."

"Come on, man! Talk to me! Make this your last truth you lying prick."

Simon put his head in his hands and started to sob. "My life can't end this way. So much time gone by and things were just starting to look up. Why now? Why would this happen to me now?" He looked up at Joe with fear in his eyes.

"What happened to YOU? Is that what you think, Simon? That this has happened to you? Funny, I thought it happened to Rita."

"But I thought it would all go away."

Just tell me what happened, Simon, for Christ's sake."

Simon stayed seated on the floor but changed his position. He stretched his legs out in front and crossed his ankles. Palms were by his side, flat on the floor. His head rested back on the cold concrete wall. He took a deep breath and began speaking.

"I was out on patrol that night, first responder mobile unit. It were a pretty cold rainy night. I had been trying to call Eva all evening but she wasn't picking up. She had just told me she was leaving me, saying she wanted a divorce. I was telling her to think about it and lets talk. It were a bad week and I was having a bad night." Simon shoulders went down slightly as his anxiety appeared to lessen. "So, then I get this call from dispatch. There was an alarm at an empty building across town, so I drove over. They wanted me to check the building, as construction was completed but was undergoing finishing touches. I couldn't see anything when I drove around the building so I parked at the front and went to check the entrance. There wasn't much light. The overhead was flickering. I saw this figure curled up in the passageway. I guessed it was a drunk trying to keep dry out of the rain. So I went up to have a look."

"And was it the girl?" Joe interrupted.

"Yes, I saw her. At first she wasn't moving."

"Did you talk to her?"

"No, she didn't really say much. I didn't know if she were sleeping or dead so I went over and shook her, to tell her to move on. I told her she couldn't be there."

"You have a big heart Simon. Was she sick?"

"I don't know if she was on drugs, I couldn't tell. There was nobody else around, just her. She was wearing a big oversized old army coat. She was half alert, shivering. I knelt down to talk to her and she suddenly latched on to me, like a magnet. She was shivering, grabbed me around the neck and was breathing in my face, in my ear. The coat fell open and she had this wee dress on. There she was, writhing around. Her dress was half way up her knickers, her leg was coming over mine. She was turning me on, you know … seductive. For all I knew she was likely a hooker anyway."

"She was fifteen you tosser!!"

"I was not to know! But she was all hanging on to me, her dress was barely there, thin like paper. Her nipples were hard and showing through her dress. She was all over me. Her breath was on my face, her lips near mine. So I held her and then I saw her knickers were showing. So I touched her there, you know, and she didn't resist, so I touched her harder. The next thing I know we're having it on. She was inviting. She wanted me, not like Eva."

"You raped her, Simon, plain and simple. You raped a sick, feverish child. Did you ever think that she was hanging on to you because she was cold?"

"No, it weren't like that, I swear. She wanted it too. She were hanging on to me and moaning. Not like Eva who said nobody would, want me. I was sure showing her!" Simon had stopped talking. He sat looking at the floor, not raising his eyes to look at Joe, who had stopped breathing.

Just when Joe thought the quiet would make his head explode, Simon started talking again.

"But then she must have fallen asleep or something, so I left her and went to do my check. I came back, and she was saying something I couldn't make it out. She started grabbing at me again."

"Maybe she was saying "help me." Did you think of that?"

"No, you should have seen her, Joe. She wanted it, I could tell. She were hot, she were as aroused as I was. She was all half naked in her wet dress, her face was pulled up to mine. Suddenly I was hard, so we did it again. I stayed with her for a while. She looked like she was asleep. When I started to move she woke up. I had to get out of there, so I told her I'd be back. She kept saying "Promise" and I said, "Yeah, yeah, I'll be back. I promise.""

"Is that what you said to her, that you promised you'd be back? That's sick," said Joe.

"Hey, I wasn't even sure she was going to be alive. Maybe she was dying. What else could I say? I couldn't just say, "Wham, bam, thank you, ma'am." When I went to my truck, dispatch had been calling me, and I panicked. I forgot to call it in when I arrived. I don't know how long they had been trying to reach me, so I said I had a flat tyre and I was too far away to get there. I radioed Gen and asked him to take the call. He radioed dispatch and said he was on his way."

Simon by now had rested his back against the wall in a subdued defeat. "I never went back. I had to make a run. Over the years I had forgotten about it. I'd moved on." Simon was no longer looking at Joe, the guilt apparent on his face and in his voice. He tried to change the subject. "I know, you and I had our wild times after that, didn't we Joe? But then I got back on track with Liz."

Joe wanted to punch him more than anything and was having a hard time not doing it.

"I didn't need this girl coming back into my life. When I saw her, it was like seeing a ghost. She scared the crap out of me."

"Rita got pregnant, Simon. It was your baby. Didn't that matter to you? Don't you think she was scared too?"

"She's a prostitute, for Christ's sake. How do I know it was mine? She was just trying to destroy my life."

"She wasn't a prostitute. She was a fifteen-year-old runaway, who didn't know where to go or who to trust. But you raped her and you got away with it. The child is yours, Simon. We've got your DNA."

"It was just sex. I'm sure that happens all the time. Besides, like I told you, it was consensual from where I was standing."

Joe thought about Aidan, hoping he would never learn that his biological father had raped and murdered his mother. "So why, after all that, did you kill her? You've insulted her twice."

"She were going to tell you … and Liz."

"How did she know about Liz?"

"She saw us together at Nonna's. She knew where I lived, man! She could have just showed up there at any time. I couldn't have that. And she knew where you lived. She said she was coming for your help. She knew you were a PI from a clipping in the paper. She had showed it to me. She said she was going to tell everyone. I didn't want to lose Liz."

"Well, you've lost us all now, mate. Liz, me, Eva, Vincent - all of us."

"I didn't mean it. Just as I was driving to your place I saw her on the road, only a block from your house. I had gone to pick you up not knowing if you had already left. When I saw your car missing, I parked near your spot and started walking towards her. I intercepted her on the roadway. She was cycling towards your driveway. We argued, and she started hitting me, the bitch. So I pulled out my blade. I meant to scare her, but she wasn't scared. So I finished it, right then and there. It had to end."

Joe sat looking at Simon, an unstoppable sadness creeping over his face. He stood up and walked to the door of the cell. He had absolutely nothing left to say to Simon, nor would he ever. He knocked on the door hard for the guard to let him out. He stumbled out of the building through the nearest fire exit and into the fresh air, not stopping to speak to anyone.

CHAPTER 48

Joe had a sleepless night. Never could he have imagined the cost of helping young Stefan. The devastation caused by broken trust was beyond all his comprehension. In flashback, Joe saw everything that was wrong, all the things he didn't see. Maybe things he didn't want to see. His memory took him back to happier days - to Endcliffe Park, walking home from school in their last year, discussing their futures. They had loved walking through the woodlands along Porter Brook, the massive oaks with their sheltering canopy from the rain or the sun.

He had a mental image of a younger Simon, on the old stone steps. Those shallow mossy ones that twisted down the grassy hillside, framed by the lush greenness of the grass. Joe's memory of the occasion was vivid beyond belief. They were with Janet and Eva, all dressed up for Janet's graduation party. Simon looked a right bobby dazzler that day. He knew how to dress up back when he was younger. What happened to Simon?

Joe's memory guided him through the years, attending each other's weddings, the birth of Susan. Simon's support and concern through Joe's divorce, his fierce loyalty when Joe castigated himself for following the wrong guy and almost dying. But he also remembered how often he had inappropriately defended Simon. He remembered his temper, his ability to go into a rage.

Simon, who had loved his wife and had come to earn the respect and admiration of his girlfriend, Liz - how could he treat a girl in a ragged dress like a piece of meat? The act was rape, and he was lying in saying he didn't see it that way. He had pent up anger against his wife, felt unjustifiably abandoned and hard done by. Simon loved to play the victim. Everything was always someone else's fault. Everyone owed him. He was the worst kind of fickle.

Joe had no misgiving about the way things ended. He had no remorse whatsoever for turning Simon in. It was his job, and it was the right thing to do. Janet was right. Simon had brought him down and held him back for most of his life. Joe had always been there to defend him, or to wallow with him. Joe was the same man, yet felt a different man, perhaps not by accident. Emotions that had lain dormant were now resurfacing. He had a renewed understanding and empathy towards others. Of Rita and Stefan and Aisha for starters. He was humbled by their courage and optimism. These were qualities he had been lacking.

Liz had refused numerous requests from Simon to go and visit him at the prison. She said she never wanted to see him again. She packed up all of her belongings, locked his door, and went back to be with her daughter. It was a dismal turn of events. It was unclear what would happen to his possessions, but nobody seemed to care. Let the authorities deal with it. Simon was dead to them.

Joe's thoughts were interrupted by the telephone. He didn't even realize that he was sitting outside in the cool sunshine. It was Stefan calling to say the Dwights had rung. They wanted him to come to Aidan's birthday party next month.

"I asked them what changed their minds. Didn't they say it was best to wait? And guess what she said, Joe? Mrs. Dwight."

"Slow down Stefan, and tell me what she said."

"Well, she said the neighbour next door had just given birth to a little girl. Aidan has been so curious about it ever since. He always wants to go and see the baby. And then suddenly, he started asking Elaine, Mrs. Dwight, about what it was like being pregnant with him. He wanted to know if he kicked a lot, and how come he doesn't have black hair like his daddy, saying the baby next door has black hair like his daddy. They didn't want to lie to the boy. So they got in touch with their adoption counselor, and support group and they spent time talking to people."

Joe carried the phone indoors. The sun was clouding over and the breeze picked up, turning it cooler. Stefan was still talking.

"These people were telling the Dwights that the best age was now, around eight years. Aidan is exceptionally mature for his age, so would have a good comprehension. He is old enough to feel secure about it. And he can understand it by now. As for explaining to Aidan what happened to his other mother, they will deal with that in time. But they said this would be a good opportunity to tell him he has an uncle. Mr. Dwight thought it might soften the news of being adopted, having a blood relative in the room."

Joe was thrilled with this news. He could hear the emotion in Stefan's voice.

Stefan went on, "I want nothing more than to be there, so I said yes. I will take some pictures, Maybe I can get a selfie of Aidan and me. Then I will tell me mum, if she lives that long. It's getting harder to see her; she's got maybe just weeks left." His voice quieted as he added, "Funny, the only three pictures I have of Rita are her Year Eight class photo, her mug shot, and her morgue photo. I could only ever show Aidan the class photo."

Not knowing how to respond to that, Joe simply said, "I'm very sorry about your mum, Stefan."

"Thank you, Joe, that means a lot to me. You've been a great friend to me. But Joe, I want to say that I am thinking of moving to Sheffield. I want to do what you do. The way you helped me … it was brilliant. You made me feel real inside. You brought me back to my sister. I was able to live her life with you, know where she had been and what she had done. If I can do that for other people, it would make me feel so good inside. Maybe it is something I could be good at."

"But you've only seen one side of it. It doesn't necessarily work out well, Stefan. Sometimes you can't find the answers. And not everybody will be pleased about what you do find."

"Yes, but think about it. All Rita wanted was to know Aidan was okay. If she had got to your place that night without Simon spotting her, you would have helped her find him. She wanted Aidan and look, you helped me find him for her. She would have been so happy to know it worked out."

Stefan paused for a moment in thought. "Okay, it doesn't always have to work out, but parts of it still do. Even a blind squirrel finds a nut once in a while. Besides, I can go to school and learn how to become a private eye, like you. I'm good at school and learning things."

Joe was not in a position to dissuade him. He knew the lad had a strong will and could choose his own future.

Hanging up the phone, Joe wondered if he and Stefan would stay in touch now that this was over. Somehow he had the feeling they would.

Over the following weeks, Joe often pictured Rita lying in that doorway being assaulted by Simon. He remembered something that Glen Whitely had said to him when he first found Rita. She had pushed at him saying 'No. no.' The attending police constable had said the same thing. The poor girl probably thought they were lining up to assault her. It was incomprehensible what she went through, yet she tried so hard to move on and to have a life. She and Stefan had the same fortitude.

If Rodney hadn't been such a crap boyfriend, she may have stayed in Barnsley and done okay. Maybe her mistake was returning to Sheffield, and in seeing that damn CORP uniform again.

CHAPTER 49

It was another snowy November morning. The sun was melting the dusting that had fallen over night but his boots left imprints in the shady areas. His life was about to change even more. A few hours ago, he had shaken the hand of the real estate agent who had put the "For Sale" sign on the front of his house. Susan had been standing beside him holding his hand, smiling encouragingly at him. She had worked hard convincing Dad it was time to sell. Meeting Aisha and seeing the look on his face when he was near her had been convincing enough. He was ready to move on.

Joe had been seeing a lot of Susan lately. Just last week, he had received a text from her. It was an odd little picture that looked like a fuzzy black-and-white TV screen with a caption that read, "Look what Nigel and I have made." Aisha explained that it was an ultrasound. She had to explain further what it meant. He had driven over to see Susan and Nigel, and they explained that it had happened quite by accident, but they were pleased about it. They didn't want it to change anything and would make the baby fit into their lives and not the other way around.

"You will likely meet my parents very soon. It's time we had them for a visit. My dad is very eager to meet you," a beaming Nigel had added. "And you can likely expect a visit from my aunt Claire. I think she'd like to meet you. Dad says she's been involved in a bit of sleuthing herself, many years ago. It was just after I was born."

Joe was in an abstracted rapture. His Susan was going to be a mom. "I am looking forward to meeting your parents, Nigel. You are right, it is time," Joe concurred, a ridiculously happy look on his face.

At this moment, Joe was walking the highest spot at Ladybower, imagining a different future, with all the changes coming. Susan and Nigel had declined the invite to come along. He sat down on a rock and peeled a banana. He closed his eyes to the comfort of the hospitable afternoon sun that was warming his face. He was trying hard to concentrate on the here and now and not on the rest of the world.

It had been another bad week in the news. Europeans were experiencing a mass uneasiness. Paris had just been under attack by terrorists. The paper said likely 100 had been killed. The attack had happened at the Bataclan concert hall of all places. An American metal band had been playing on stage at the time. There were rumours circulating that roughly six of the hall's security guards didn't show up for duty that night, perhaps being ISIS terrorists themselves and assisting the attackers. ISIS had claimed responsibility but would neither confirm nor deny the allegation that security guards were involved. The truth might never come out, but in the end it doesn't really matter. Joe remembered the comment Susan had made on their hike to Ladybower some weeks ago, about people loving their pets more than humans. The profundity of those comments hit him now with astonishing clarity.

Although he tried hard not to, his thoughts did occasionally turn to Simon. He would sit in a cell until his trial, and for his crimes he would undoubtedly receive a mandatory life sentence. But Joe didn't want to think of Simon. He wanted to think of Rita. Rita and Simon had a son. That was the incredibly bizarre ending to this tragedy. Joe wondered how Aidan would turn out. Hopefully he would inherit the best traits of his parents, before life dealt them each a bad hand. Aidan had a better chance of success. He had a wonderful family, and he had Stefan. Joe had no doubt that the lad could influence Aidan in a positive way. Life had changed for a lot of people, all for Rita wanting Aidan.

Joe had been seated in his office a few days later when Andrew King knocked on his door.

"Sorry to bother you, Mr. Parrott. I just thought you'd like to see this. It's a note she left me, the day she went to your house. She and I were planning to meet after work and go for a meal, but she didn't come. It's why I went looking for her." He handed Joe a folded piece of notepaper. "It's of no use to me any more, and I thought you could decide if you wanted to give it to her brother. Bye, Mr. Parrott. Sorry I didn't help sooner."

He didn't open it until after Andrew had left. There in her own writing were the words that told her side of the story.

"Hi Andrew, I know you'll be pissed coz you told me not to go. I'm sorry I've been so angry and all. But ever since I saw the uniform, then him, all the memories came back. It happened a long time ago. I wos stupid and so scared. I know wot he did to me, 'cause I know wot me dad did to me. Me dad says it wos because he loved me. That's what love is, he said. That wos bollocks but this wos worse. I remember that night. It was chucking it down and I was sick and cold. At first I didn't know what he wos doing, I thought I wos dreaming. I thought that he loved me, the way he was acting. He said he'd be back. I know he wronged me, like me dad. That's bang out of order. I never did nothing bad to nobody so why'd he do this to me? But Andrew, I know where that Joe Parrott lives. I have to go see him and tell him. He can tell me if my baby is safe. He can make that man pay to help me find my baby. It's only right he do that. Then we can get on with it, right Andrew? I'll see you later, leave the light on.

Love, your Rita."

As Joe sat lost in his thoughts he felt the gentle squeeze to his hand. He looked over and Aisha was smiling at him, shaking her head. This woman had become such a meaningful part of his life ... this enchanting being, who looked at him in a way that was compelling him to move forward with his life. His heart was overwhelmed with affection and gratitude.

"You're thinking again," she suggested as she wrapped her arms lovingly around his neck.

"I feel old", he said as he put his arms around her waist. He looked into her eyes and smiled.

Nudging him playfully, she said, "Yes, but you're never too old to be magnificent."

NONNA'S

I would like to thank the owner at Nonna's in Sheffield, Maurizio Mori, who has generously allowed me to use not only his establishment but also this photo. A trip to Sheffield is not complete without a trip to Nonna's.

I would like to thank my husband David, for his help with some of the Yorkshire vocabulary. Also I would again like to thank Frank Giampa, for his enthusiasm and encouragement. I couldn't ask for a better advocate. I would never have picked up a pen if it weren't for him.

NOTE FROM THE AUTHOR

I thoroughly enjoyed writing *Wanting Aidan* and I hope you enjoyed reading it. Throughout the writing process, the story took a few unexpected turns, as I'm sure happens. Being new to this, it came as a pleasant surprise and made me realize just how strong my love of writing has become.

Nigel was incorporated into the story quite by accident, but it was an easy fit. In my third book, *Romero Pools,* Nigel again returns, as do other familiar characters from both *Trusting Claire* and *Wanting Aidan.* They will all become connected in creative fashion. While my books are stand-alone, you as the reader have the opportunity to learn more about the characters by reading *Trusting Claire.*

Again I want to thank you for reading my book. Please help me further by submitting a review on Amazon or Good Reads. These reviews are valuable in getting my name out there. No writer can continue to write if there are no readers, so what you say matters.

Please watch for my next book, *Romero Pools,* which will be available by the end of 2021.

www.alyhallwriter.com

Trusting Claire by Alyssa Hall

What readers are saying about this book on Amazon.ca:

5.0 out of 5 stars

Great debut full of sharp observations. Can't wait for a next book!

Reviewed in Canada on December 23, 2020

It's incredible how many interesting and vivid details the author was able to put in the relatively small package. Her writing is full of life and allows to create a complete visual about places and characters. The expressive language brings out so many emotions without you being mired in the unnecessary. I love how the author introduces the characters and gives you a chance to travel in time and experience different cultures and places. This is a great debut full of sharp observations about the world, the human nature and relationships, the lives of immigrants and their children and more. This book is delicious to read and I can't wait for a next book by Alyssa Hall.

5.0 out of 5 stars

Amazing read. Can't wait for her next book.

Reviewed in Canada on March 12, 2021

I read my fair share of mysteries and while I enjoy the genre, I find many mysteries are marred by overly complex and gimmicky plot twists. In this respect, Alyssa Hall's Trusting Claire is a refreshing and original antidote. Hall's narrative style is subtle and restrained, allowing the suspense of the story to build organically rather than being forced. Her approach does not attempt to manipulate the reader. Her deft characterization of Claire's relationships, both romantic and platonic, transported me back to my twenties when seemingly inconsequential choices can change the course of our lives. I highly recommend this book and look forward to her upcoming novel.

4.0 out of 5 stars
Trusting Claire by Alyssa Hall
Reviewed in Canada on January 19, 2021

Alyssa Hall has written a nifty page-turner about relatable characters in a small-town living in the shadow of a murder. Hall's robust imagination lets loose as Claire investigates the mysterious and troubled man she was dating, She won't take no for an answer and threats of danger make her even more determined, and that makes her a hero. Hall's appealing debut is a winner. Hope she's writing another

5.0 out of 5 stars
Captivating and Mysterious..
Reviewed in Canada on February 1, 2021

Trusting Claire was a wonderful read and I thoroughly enjoyed it. Alyssa did a great job at painting such a descriptive picture for her readers and making them feel a part of Claire's journey. I would recommend this to all of my friends, family, and peers. Can't wait to see what Alyssa has is store for us next!

5.0 out of 5 stars
<u>An interesting read.</u>
Reviewed in Canada on February 6, 2021

Her first novel moves along at a nice easy pace. References to Russian immigrants and enjoying life in Greece, makes it a good read.

Back in Canada her life changes dramatically involving a murder mystery.

5.0 out of 5 stars
<u>Must Read</u>
Reviewed in Canada on March 8, 2021

Very much enjoyed reading this author's first book, very well written, keeps you engaged. This is a great book to add to my library. Looking forward to her next book. Well done for a first time author!

CPSIA information can be obtained
at www.ICGtesting.com
Printed in the USA
LVHW091633130621
690121LV00008B/1549

9 781039 104808